THE COACHMAN'S DAUGHTER

Donna Creekmore

After her sister's mysterious disappearance Linnet Hamilton returned to her native England and to Ashwood, her orphaned niece's home. From the moment she arrived, Sean Carlisle, steward of the estate, seemed able to read Linnet's every thought. Why did he want her to stay? Could the reason be because he had a sinister dream of possessing Ashwood? Or was there another reason that might forever link Linnet, a mere coachman's daughter, with Sean, Lord of the Manor, the man she was beginning to believe she loved?

Also in Large Print
by
Donna Creekmore

The Difficult Miss Livingston

THE COACHMAN'S DAUGHTER

Donna Creekmore

Curley Publishing, Inc.
South Yarmouth, Ma.

-L
F
CRE

CADCC

EH RD SR DW

Library of Congress Cataloging-in-Publication Data

Creekmore, Donna.
  The coachman's daughter / Donna Creekmore.
    p. cm.
  1. Large type books.   I. Title.
  [PS3553.R338C74 1991]
  813'.54—dc20
  ISBN 0–7927–0925–X (lg. print)   90–25475
  ISBN 0–7927–0926–8 (pbk: lg. print)   CIP

Published in Large Print by arrangement with Donald MacCampbell, Inc. in the United States, Canada, the U.K. and British Commonwealth and the rest of the world market.

Distributed in Great Britain, Ireland and the Commonwealth by CHIVERS LIBRARY SERVICES LIMITED, Bath BA1 3HB, England.

Printed in Great Britain

THE COACHMAN'S DAUGHTER

ONE

My childhood consisted of two nearly equal parts, and Father spent the better portion of the second reminding me of the first.

"You are *not* a Coachman's Daughter," he would begin.

This conversation ordinarily took place while we were dining at the round mahogany table in our sitting room. Father would slam his fist on the marble top, covered with a linen cloth at mealtimes, and the dishes, silverware, and serving pieces would rattle as if to confirm his pronouncement. However, as Father was usually clad in his livery – the black trousers and scarlet coat which proclaimed him a servant of Phelps Parker – I would find it difficult to believe either him or the clamoring cutlery.

"You are not a Coachman's Daughter," he would repeat, as if reading my skepticism. "You are a Gentlewoman. You must never forget, never, that your family was one of the most aristocratic in England. You were born at Hamilton Oaks –"

And then Father would launch into what I came to term The Litany. He would start

1

with the estate itself – the redbrick Stuart manor house, the parks and gardens, the rich tenant farms in the English county of Norfolk. He would describe the house in glowing superlatives that corresponded but vaguely with my own memories, for I recalled it as dark, drafty, and perennially cold. Nor were our recollections of the gardens the same. He apparently saw them as they had been in his youth – perfectly pruned and manicured – while I visualized them as they had appeared at the end, after the gardeners had been released, with straggling hedges and armies of encroaching weeds. Only when he spoke of the farms – Greenfields in particular – would I feel a stab of nostalgia. For I, too, remembered Mrs. Carter – young in Father's time, old in mine – and her inexhaustible offerings of newly baked bread and fresh, warm milk.

When I was young, it disturbed me that Father's memories seemed so impersonal, that the physical trappings of that other life weighed more heavily in his mind than we, his family. Later, I understood that Hamilton Oaks was a symbol of all that had been lost and that Father found it less painful to discuss the gabled manor house and once-lush gardens than to talk of Mother and Robin and me. For when he broached that subject, near the

2

middle of his discourse, there was invariably a tremor in his voice.

"How happy we were," he would say, delicately patting his lips with his napkin. "Your mother and I and our two beautiful daughters. Robin and Linnet, the songbirds of Hamilton Oaks."

If I was in a rebellious frame of mind, as I often was during my adolescence, I would wonder irritably about Father's "songbirds." Had he selected the names before Robin and I were born? Or had "Robin" suggested itself by accident, to be followed – after seven years and great deliberation – with "Linnet"? What would he have named a son? "Jay" perhaps?

I never asked these questions because my role in The Litany was carefully circumscribed. After Father's initial reminiscences about Mother and his songbirds, it was time for me to say:

"Tell me about *your* childhood, Father. Tell me what it was like when you and Aunt Jane were growing up."

Father would nearly have finished his main course by then and would lay his fork aside. "Ah, those were golden days indeed," he would say and would then embark upon the lengthy recital that proved his contention.

I supposed, as I reluctantly absorbed the fundamentals of English history, that they *had* been golden days for a child of the landed gentry: the 1840's and 1850's. Miss Benton explained that agriculture was then the cornerstone of the English economy, often drawing parallels between England and her home state of Mississippi. But Father was grandly unconcerned with the inevitable tides of history and focused on the trees rather than the forest.

He paraded forth a long string of governesses (which I perceived as a long string of Miss Bentons) and detailed the nasty pranks he and Aunt Jane had played upon them. He described their romps through the vast parklands of Hamilton Oaks, their visits to Greenfields. He recounted his experiences in public school, his adventures at the university. He mentioned the London town house his father had let for the season of Aunt Jane's coming-out. He concluded this part of The Litany with the doleful reminder that – as a result of this wretched season in London – Aunt Jane had married into Trade.

Father's reiteration of Aunt Jane's fall from grace was timed to coincide with the completion of the entrée. At this point Father would unveil his dessert and might or might not inaugurate the second portion of The Litany. I learned, as the years passed, that if the dessert was something Father favored (pudding or custard), he would consume it in silence. If not, he would address the question of how we had come to lose Hamilton Oaks.

Did I say he addressed the question? Actually, he talked very skilfully around it. He mumbled about the repeal of the Corn Laws in 1846, an event Miss Benton had touched on during one of her interminable English history lessons. He complained – still in a mumble – that this parliamentary lapse had opened a Pandora's box of cheap grain imports. He mournfully listed the tenant farms in the order of their disposal: Riverside, Oakland, Forest View, Greenfields.

"Then your mother died," he would say, shoving his brandied fruit or mince pie away, "and I was forced to sell Hamilton Oaks as well."

I was better than half-grown – fifteen or sixteen – when I detected the holes in Father's narrative and filled them in for myself. I realized that Mother's death could not have precipitated a sudden financial crisis at Hamilton Oaks. On Father's free evenings he rushed out of our quarters just after dinner and did not return till well after midnight. The next day he stomped about and cursed the peculiarities of a faro game or roulette wheel. Father, I concluded, was and always had been a gambler. He had lost

5

the tenant farms but clung to the manor house, discharging the servants as necessary. Mother's death had broken his spirit, and he had surrendered Hamilton Oaks, settling his debts and severing his ties with England in one fell swoop.

But this theory, like my doubts about the songbirds, remained unvoiced, for the reference to Mother would wrinkle Father's forehead, purse his lips, and set him to studying me.

"You look just like her, you know," he would say. He would rise and walk to the walnut table that sat beside the sofa. He would pick up the framed painting of Mother and gaze at it. "Just like her," he would repeat.

I was intimately familiar with the painting because I wore a miniature of it inside a cameo locket. I would open my locket, and Father would remind me that it was the duplicate of one left with Robin in England. His mother had been a twin . . .

I would close my ears to his digression and examine the tiny portrait. I would see a thin, almost gaunt face with smooth, fair skin seemingly stretched over the prominent cheekbones. A short, straight nose; an overly sharp chin. Black hair parted in the center and arranged in the loose chignon of the 1860's.

6

Lips a trifle too small; enormous violet eyes, which compensated for the deficiencies of mouth and chin. The resemblance became clear by the time I was thirteen and increased with every year thereafter.

"You're considerably taller than she, of course," Father would say. I was never certain whether this was a criticism or merely a comment. "Robin – now Robin is tiny. Robin is *exactly* like your mother."

I knew this to be true, for I remembered Robin as she had been when Father and I left England. I was eleven then and Robin eighteen. I had seen her but once during the years just prior to our departure, for at fourteen she had gone to London to live with Aunt Jane while attending school. (Evidently, Father had elected, under the circumstances, to risk the nefarious influence of Trade.) Father occasionally proposed a family excursion to the city or murmured that he really must send the fare so Robin could come home between terms. But she spent only one Christmas in Norfolk, and I later surmised that Father's discretionary income had shrunk virtually to nothing, prohibiting even so modest a luxury as a jaunt between London and Hamilton Oaks.

At any rate, when Robin arrived in Norfolk the day after Mother's death, she was not

7

the plumpish adolescent I had kicked and scratched and screamed at. She was a woman – short and slim, raven-haired and lavender-eyed. And if Father doubted her maturity, his doubt was short-lived. Four weeks later, when we stopped in London to fetch Robin for the journey to America, she announced her engagement to Justin Ashworth.

Father had no reason to oppose the marriage. Justin was the second son of a distinguished Surrey family, and a medical student. I don't believe Father had any clear idea of what he might do in America – indeed, where he might go in that sprawling land. He must have assumed Robin would fare better as an English matron than, perhaps, as a victim of "the heathen savages who infest the western territories."

Father was disappointed, as I was, that we had no opportunity to meet Justin. But Father had scheduled our emigration with characteristic abruptness – booking our passage just five days before the ship was to sail – and Justin had been called to Ashwood, his home in Surrey. His father was extremely ill, Robin explained (in fact, he was to die within a few days), and Justin could not leave Sir Robert's bedside. Aunt Jane grudgingly conceded that Justin was "a respectable young man," Uncle Henry pronounced him "a good-natured chap," and Father was forced to settle for this vicarious approval of his future son-in-law.

"At least," he said, as we boarded the train for Southampton, "your sister has not got embroiled with a Tradesman."

"Your mother was a wonderful woman." As often as we intoned The Litany, Father's words never failed to startle me from my reverie. "A splendid woman. Half Irish, but a lady nevertheless. If she were home, she would counsel you as I do. She would remind you that breeding is everything. She would caution you not to forget your background. She would tell you you are *not* a Coachman's Daughter."

And thus The Litany would end as it had begun. Father would replace Mother's portrait on the table, and I would be excused, secure in the knowledge that the conversation would recur a week, a fortnight, a month, hence.

While I would never have confessed it to Father, I had grave reservations about The Litany, for I could scarcely imagine circumstances preferable to mine. I adored being a Coachman's Daughter; my life, it seemed to me, bordered on perfection.

I never learned the precise sequence of events that brought Father into Phelps

Parker's household, but I feel, in retrospect, that gambling lent a hand. When we reached New York, Father hired a cab, which delivered us to a tumbledown house in a seedy Irish neighborhood. We would stay, he said, with a "distant cousin of your mother" until Father found employment and suitable lodgings. The "distant cousin" bore a suspicious resemblance to a former groom at Hamilton Oaks, but he, his stout wife, and seven children were very kind to us.

Several years elapsed before it occurred to me that Father's method of seeking employment had been rather unorthodox. He slept until late afternoon or early evening, cheerfully snoring in the double bed he and I shared with the O'Rourkes' youngest child. He rose at five or six, took dinner, and left the house. I woke once or twice when he returned and sleepily observed gray tendrils of dawn creeping through the window and across the crowded bedroom.

Be that as it may, Father shook me awake in the dim light of an early morning to inform me that he had secured a position. We were to leave the very next day for Chicago, Illinois, where Father would become Mr. Phelps Parker's coachman. Did Mr. Parker, who was known to be a gambler himself, "win" Father in a poker game? Or did they happen to meet in one of New York's better gambling establishments? I don't know, but I am certain that Chance, in some form, propelled us across the country to the city on Lake Michigan.

We were met at the LaSalle Street Station by one of Mr. Parker's numerous grooms, who drove us to the Parker mansion on Lake Shore Drive. Mansion, I say: it was a veritable castle, with towers round and square, thrusting chimneys, wings sprouting in every direction. The interior of the house exceeded my wildest imaginings: marble floors, soaring ebony staircases, frescoed ceilings, silver-inlaid paneling. To augment my ecstasy, the house was equipped with indoor plumbing and steam heat, luxuries I had not previously enjoyed. I decided at once that the Parker house was a distinct cut above Hamilton Oaks, an opinion I did not, of course, share with Father.

Phelps Parker was about forty when Father entered his employ – a blond giant of a man, reputed to be the wealthiest and most powerful in Chicago. He owned the city's principal department store and finest hotel and had extensive holdings in the meat-packing industry, the railroads, the western mines. The only amenity he lacked – prior to that summer of 1880 – was a British coachman. I believe he was extremely pleased to acquire Father's services, for he accorded him, and me, unusual privileges.

First of all, we were not assigned rooms in the warren of servants' quarters on the fourth story; we were granted a suite – a sitting room and two bedrooms – in one of the guest wings. Nor were we asked to take our meals in the kitchen with the rest of the staff; a kitchen maid brought them to our sitting room and removed the soiled dishes when we had finished. Father was given access to Mr. Parker's mahogany-paneled library and the freedom to leave the premises almost at will.

More important in my view, Father was allowed to include me in most of his activities. I fairly lived in the coach yard, my nose gradually adjusting to the smell of horses, which mingled with the pervasive stench of the stockyards far to the south. Father taught me to hitch the horses to the various rigs and then to drive them. The most exciting times were those when we took out Mr. Parker's celebrated chestnut trotters. We would harness the trotters to a surrey if the weather was mild, to a sleigh in winter, and strut along Lake Shore Drive as though we were still the Hamiltons of Hamilton Oaks.

I had one personal privilege I would joyfully have relinquished: Miss Benton. Miss Benton was governess to the three obstreperous Parker children, and it was Mrs. Parker who suggested to Father that I join her brood in the third-floor schoolroom. I felt I was quite sufficiently educated, but Father hastened to accept Mrs. Parker's offer, and five mornings a week I trudged into the family wing to be bludgeoned with Knowledge.

Miss Benton was of medium height, and her severely corseted waist tended to emphasize her bountiful bosom. She had dark-brown hair, and during the early weeks of our acquaintance I puzzled over its odd arrangement. Then I saw her with her hair down (Samuel Parker and I invaded her bedroom to plant a toad and caught her in her dressing gown) and realized that her outlandish coiffure was designed to hide abundant streaks of gray. Shortly after that, Miss Benton apparently obtained some sort of magic potion because the gray disappeared and she adopted a conventional hairstyle.

Miss Benton, as she pointed out at least once per day, came from Mississippi. No subject was too remote to prompt a stream of reminiscences about her life in the pre-War South. If we were studying mathematics, Miss Benton would calculate in cotton bales. If we were discussing natural science, Miss Benton would describe the exotic plants

13

and animals on her father's plantation. And history – history consisted not of battles and presidents but of Miss Benton's thrilling, tragic experiences.

I eventually pieced Miss Benton's tales together and deduced that she had been reared on the grandest cotton plantation in Mississippi; that all her male relatives had been killed in the recent civil conflict; that she and her aged mother had been expelled from their sun-swept, white-columned palace; and that Miss Benton – not a whit daunted by her multiple misfortunes – had marched upon Chicago, boldly seeking her fortune in the very heartland of the enemy. However, I subsequently overheard two of the maids in sniggering conversation, the gist of which was that Miss Benton had once been a *"very close friend"* of Phelps Parker.

Whatever her background, or lack thereof, Miss Benton was an insignificant thorn in my side. We had class each weekday from eight until twelve, at which time our lunch was delivered by a trio of kitchen maids. The Parker children then adjourned to specialized lessons – accounting or economics for Samuel; dancing, music, or drawing for the girls. Miss Benton instructed the girls in art, and I attended two or three sessions. But I hadn't a smidgin of talent, and Father and Miss

14

Benton quickly agreed that neither I nor the Parker daughters stood to benefit from my continued participation.

So at one o'clock I raced to the stables to join Father. Occasionally, I arrived before he had completed his morning duty: driving Mrs. Parker to her Calls. But he was never far behind me, and in the afternoon we would exercise the trotters or run errands or try out a new horse. Sometimes I accompanied Father when he brought Mr. Parker home from work. I thought the big, jovial man grew rather fond of me, for he often asked me to sit with him inside the coach, where he regaled me with tales of his boyhood in Ohio.

This halcyon existence lasted for five years, until just after my seventeenth birthday. I had fallen into the habit of borrowing Mrs. Parker's fashion magazines, and I did occasionally fret over my appearance. I studied the latest coiffures and bonnets and deplored my own bare head and undisciplined hair. I admired the gowns – magnificently bustled – and lamented my shapeless, outmoded dresses, which always seemed an inch or two too short. But on the whole I was supremely happy – a Coachman's Daughter who aspired to no other position in all the world.

Disaster struck late in the summer of

1885; Father married Miss Benton, whom I was instructed henceforth to refer to as "Clara." Superficially, Father's nuptials improved my situation. We moved to larger quarters – a suite comprising a handsome sitting room, two bedrooms, and a study. Our meals became feasts, for Clara was audacious enough to demand delicacies usually reserved for the family. In view of my age and new relationship with Clara, I was dismissed forever from the schoolroom. These advantages notwithstanding, I was profoundly miserable.

Lonely to begin with. Clara revamped her schedule to conform with Father's, and I watched helplessly as *she* rode out behind the great chestnut trotters, as *she* went to fetch Mr. Parker from his department store, his hotel, his LaSalle Street office. Father had always discouraged me from befriending the maids, the grooms, the stable boys, and I was too old to associate with the Parker children. So I spent most of my time immersed in Mrs. Parker's magazines, whose elegant sketches in no way bolstered my sagging morale.

Then there was The Litany, which Clara slowly throttled. I never determined what it was she resented about it. Father's memories of Mother, whose portrait had been hidden away? His memories of Hamilton Oaks, which challenged hers of Rosemont Plantation? His memories of England? No, Clara was too unrepentant a rebel to suffer even a twinge of patriotism on behalf of the newly reunited states.

At any rate, she sat through the ceremony once or twice, then began to gnaw at it.

"Oh, really, John, must we? I'm sure Linnet has heard that story a thousand times. Linnet is an *American* now. Linnet must learn to appreciate the heritage of her adopted country."

"The heritage of her adopted country," meaning the lore of antebellum Mississippi. Clara would now describe the endless cotton fields under her father's plows, the hordes of Negro slaves who had jumped at the merest crook of her finger, the balls and house parties that had studded that bygone era. After several months of this, I entertained myself by keeping track of Clara's discrepancies. She had coyly claimed to be twenty-eight when she and Father married. How was it that she remembered "reading" of the secession of South Carolina? She would have been three. Even more astonishing, she had apparently, during her infancy, danced the night away with a succession of eager suitors. Eventually, I could not resist calling her hand.

"You say this ball was in 1859, Clara?

Weren't you a trifle young to be attending balls?"

"I'm afraid you misunderstood, Linnet, dear," she said coolly, brushing a too-dark curl off her forehead. "That particular ball was one my sister told me of."

It was the first time Clara had mentioned a sister, but I saw no point in belaboring the issue.

I had squirmed through The Litany, doubted it, silently derided it, but it had been a mainstay of my life, and I felt as though a rug had been torn from under me. And Clara was no more inclined to discuss the English present than the English past. She openly sulked whenever Father spoke of Robin, but I believed I knew the reason for this. Robin had made Clara a step-grandmother, which did not enhance Clara's frantically perpetrated image of eternal youth.

Robin had married Justin Ashworth in 1882 and had borne him a daughter, Mercy, in 1883. For several years following her marriage Robin's monthly letters radiated happiness and optimism. Justin had purchased a "charming" three-storied house in Spring Street, which Robin "adored." His practice was growing "at leaps and bounds." Mercy was "a lovely, dark elf and terribly bright, at least in the eyes of her doting parents." It

18

was not until late in 1888 that the timbre of Robin's letters began to change.

Evidently, Justin's practice had expanded out of hand, for Robin complained that he was often gone in the evening: "I never know when he might return, if at all." There were thinly veiled hints that he had fallen victim to alcohol: "I sometimes hide his brandy, but he always manages to ferret it out." Nor was Justin any longer the "good-natured chap" Uncle Henry had described to us in London: "I dare not question him about his absences because he flies into a frightful rage. I pray he will not lose his temper with Mercy; I shudder to ponder the consequences."

"I don't like it," Father growled, midway through 1889. "I don't like it at all. I believe I shall write Robin and suggest they emigrate."

"And what would that accomplish?" Clara snapped, clearly uninspired by the prospect of a granddaughter tugging at her skirts. "Justin would still be a physician, and I'm sure he would find our American brandy eminently suitable." This with a glare at Father, who had been known, on occasion, to overimbibe himself.

"London is such a *violent* place," Father said. "Apparently, Jack the Ripper has departed the scene, but this madman they call the Shoreditch Slasher threatens to outperform his predecessor." Father gestured toward the scattered pages of the *Daily News*, which contained a detailed account of the latest grisly murder.

"I doubt Robin has anything to fear from the Shoreditch Slasher," I said soothingly. "He seems to prefer ladies of an altogether different class."

Father frowned; young Gentlewomen were not supposed to know of, much less discuss, the legions of prostitutes who walked the streets of London.

Though I felt a distant sympathy for Robin, I could not generate the proper sisterly concern about her problems. As the decade drew to a close and I celebrated my twenty-first birthday, I had problems of my own.

The sitting room and study, which lay between our bedrooms, muffled but could not conceal Father and Clara's incessant quarrels. The subject of their arguments was drearily predictable: Father's gambling.

He had given it up during the early months of their marriage, devoting his evenings to the interminable chess games Clara so fancied. But he had soon tired of such tame sport and had started going out again – once or twice a week in the beginning, later nearly every night. He frequented a gambling house called The Place, and his mien the following day faithfully revealed whether he had won or lost. He generally lost.

I don't think Clara viewed gambling as a vice; she had often mentioned her father's devotion to poker. Nor do I believe she envisioned imminent financial ruin; our bed and board were provided, and she had her own income. I suspect she was simply jealous of the glittering woman who had so utterly captivated Father: Lady Luck.

Be that as it may, I would ordinarily be jarred awake in the early hours of the morning by Clara's strident query: "Do you have any idea of the time?" For two or three minutes I would hear only Clara – questioning, reproving, denouncing. Then Father's voice would rise to meet hers, and I would fall uneasily back to sleep amidst a barrage of charges and recriminations and invectives.

If these nocturnal battles were not sufficiently distracting, I was also involved in my first romance. Ben Tyler was a tall, lean man with straw-colored hair and bright blue eyes. He was Phelps Parker's head gardener, and it was rumored among the maids that he was the illegitimate son of a meat-packing magnate. Whether or not these rumors were true, Ben was keenly intelligent and fiercely ambitious.

21

"And to think you're already head gardener," I said admiringly the day I shamelessly set my cap for Ben. "And you're only –"

"Twenty-six."

"Twenty-six. You must have quite a way with flowers. Trees. Hedges. All kinds of plants." Mrs. Parker's magazines had improved my appearance by then but had not nurtured me in the art of scintillating conversation.

"This is nothing." Ben's disdainful gesture encompassed the flower beds, the disciplined woods, the artificial waterfall.

"Nothing," I protested. "Why, these must be the finest gardens in Chicago. Maybe in the entire country."

"Maybe. But I intend to have my own business one day. Do you know what's happening, Linnet? Houses are going up everywhere." Another wave of his brown hand. "And houses need gardens. I save every cent of my wages" – his threadbare shirt and trousers confirmed this – "and in five years I'll have enough to start a landscaping company. I'll probably be a millionaire," he added modestly.

On this encouraging note, I began pursuing Ben Tyler in earnest. It wasn't long before "my" business became "our" business.

"You'll never want for anything," Ben assured me fervently after two or three months. "It'll be hard in the beginning, but then –" His shrug promised limitless joy and prosperity.

I don't know how long this dalliance might have continued without Father's intervention. As it was, Ben and I went for a stroll one evening after dinner, and Father – who was hitching a rig for his nightly pilgrimage to The Place – observed our first kiss, which occurred behind the stable. Father trotted off in a huff, returned in a very trice, and came to my bedroom.

"Ben Tyler is a fine young man," he began solemnly. I nodded eager agreement. "A fine young man. He has discussed his plans with me on several occasions, and I believe he'll prove successful. However" – Father gazed at his long, slender hands – "the fact remains that Ben is a servant."

As you are, I thought. Father's eyes flickered back to mine, and I noticed how old he looked. He was not yet fifty-two, but his hair was completely white, his blue eyes faded, his body stooped and much too thin.

"You are of legal age, Linnet, and I cannot prevent your marrying Ben Tyler if that is your desire. But I beg you to remember who

23

and what you are. I beg you not to demean your heritage."

Father turned and left the room, realizing, I am certain, that his quiet plea had been more effective than any conceivable tirade.

If I had loved Ben Tyler, I suppose I would have defied Father. But what I felt for Ben wasn't Love, wasn't, at least, the heart-stopping passion depicted in the novels I read. I stopped meeting Ben in the gardens, and while I missed his companionship, I was more relieved than bereft by the abrupt termination of our relationship.

Nevertheless, Father's words had aggravated a misgiving, one which had long simmered in the back of my mind. What was I? I lived among servants, yet I had no duties of my own. What would become of me when Mr. Parker's bounty ceased, as surely it must? Father insisted I was a Gentlewoman; was I destined then to be a governess, to follow in Clara's footsteps? Mrs. Parker's personal maid was elderly and ailing; might I be tapped for that position? If my future did not lie with Ben Tyler, where did it lie?

I was still contemplating these questions in the early spring of 1890 when Robin wrote to announce that she had been widowed.

Justin had gone to Ashwood to visit his family. You will remember that Lady Margaret suffered a stroke several months ago, and Edward, Justin's older brother, has also been ill. Justin had been in Surrey but two days when he went riding, and the coroner reconstructed the accident as follows: Justin returned to the stable, lit a cigar, and fell asleep. The cigar ignited a nearby pile of hay, and the stable burned to the ground within minutes. The body, I am told, was rendered quite unrecognizable by the flames, Justin's watch and brandy flask serving as the means of identification.

Robin went on to describe the funeral and concluded with the comment that Mercy was adjusting admirably to her father's death. Overall, the tone of the letter seemed one of deliverance rather than grief.

Two weeks later, in mid-April, I was puttering about our sitting room when one of the grooms barged, wild-eyed, through the door.

"It's your pa, Miss Hamilton," he panted. "Down at the stable. He done keeled over, and he told me to get you —"

I raced across the grounds behind him, distantly recalling the hundreds, thousands, of times I had come this way before. I believe

I knew, even before I saw Father, that this time would be the last.

He lay on the stable floor, a pillow of straw stuffed haphazardly beneath his head, one hand clutching his chest, his face ashen and twisted with pain.

"Linnet."

His voice was so low I could scarcely hear him, and I knelt beside him, my eyes filling with tears.

"The sofa," he gasped. "Look in the sofa." He stopped and fought for breath. "Go back to England. Promise me you'll go back to England."

His words did not register. He was all I had, all I had had for half my life, and he was leaving me. I took his hand, as though I might somehow lead him away from the brink of death.

"Promise, Linnet," he muttered hoarsely, his eyes beginning to glaze. "Promise."

"I promise, Father," I choked.

I squeezed his hand, but he was beyond response. He twitched once and emitted a stifled moan, and then his hand went limp in mine. John Hamilton had died a Coachman.

Mr. Parker declared a week of mourning, and the household plunged into mandatory gloom. Father was laid out in the main parlor – draped in black for the occasion –

and Clara and I greeted dozens of callers, most of them, I suspected, Father's gambling cronies. Mr. Parker arranged a splendid funeral and purchased a plot in the city's foremost cemetery. Upon our return from the interment, I assisted Clara – who had worked herself into a state of near-prostration – up to our quarters and collapsed in Father's favorite armchair. A few minutes later a kitchen maid brought up a steaming cup of tea and a letter from Robin.

I had debated whether to cable Robin of Father's death and had decided that a letter, though belated, would be kinder. Now I opened her letter, resolutely ignoring the melodramatic sobs that issued from Clara's bedroom.

"One tragedy follows another," Robin began. "Justin's brother, Edward, has succumbed to his illness, a blood disorder, I understand. Though I hardly knew him, my heart aches for Lady Margaret. How awful that she has lost both sons in under a month."

There were several paragraphs of trivia, growing increasingly disjointed, as though Robin was postponing some inevitable unpleasantness. Then:

"I have been glancing over my journal and am most distressed. I really cannot determine what to do."

27

I frowned. Why should Robin, reviewing her journal, find entries that had not disturbed her when she wrote them? It made no sense, but her agitation was unmistakable.

"I am quite alone," she continued, "and long for you and Linnet. If only you could come to England!"

England. I dropped the letter, suddenly recalling Father's and my final conversation. England. I had promised Father to go back to England. How? How was I, an Impoverished Gentlewoman, to finance such an undertaking? The sofa. Father had mentioned the sofa . . .

I stood up, cocked an ear toward Clara's room, and was reassured by a noisy cadence of sniffles. I crossed the sitting room to the red-velvet sofa. "Look *in* the sofa," Father had said. I ran my hand between the seat cushion and the thickly padded back and felt a wad of paper. I drew it out and beheld the fruits of Father's last, successful visit to The Place.

I don't think I would have regarded my deathbed vow as binding, but I had every reason to honor it. There was no future for me in Mr. Parker's turreted mansion; in Chicago; in all that great, raw country. Robin needed me, and I was curious to see my homeland again. I had wondered what I was; perhaps Father had left me the means to discover my identity.

If Clara noticed my sudden affluence, she didn't choose to mention it. Swathed in black, she had taken to wandering – wet-eyed – about the house, graciously acknowledging the commiserations of family and servants alike. Mr. Parker seemed particularly solicitous, and I believe Clara anticipated a renewal of their "friendship."

Clara being thus immersed in glamorous widowhood, I was able to make my arrangements without interruption. Mrs. Parker lent me the services of her seamstress, whom I commissioned to make three dresses – one black, one gray, one blue – which was all I felt I could afford. I booked passage on a ship from New York to Southampton and cabled Robin the date and hour of my arrival.

Three weeks after Father's death, Mr. Parker seated me in his finest carriage, and I waved farewell to the household, which had assembled in the circular drive to witness my departure. When we reached the LaSalle Street Station, I suffered a moment of panic. A chapter of my life had begun here, and now it was drawing to a close. The Parkers, Clara, Ben Tyler – they were not without their faults, but they were familiar. What awaited me at the end of my long journey? Surely Mr.

Parker had an acquaintance who would take me on as governess . . . The groom assisted me from the coach and signaled a porter to carry my trunk and portmanteau into the station, and I squared my shoulders. I would not dwell on endings. I was going back to England. I was going Home.

I stopped briefly in New York to visit the O'Rourkes and a cousin of Clara's; the latter confirmed my suspicion that Clara was "forty-five if she's a day." The Atlantic crossing was so uneventful as to be tedious, and after we had sighted land, I stood on deck, entertaining a new fear. Would I recognize Robin? I opened my cameo locket, studied the portrait inside, and relaxed. If Robin was still "exactly like" Mother, I would have no difficulty.

Nevertheless, I descended the gangway very slowly, jostled and grumbled at by the passengers behind me. My eyes swept the sea of expectant faces on the dock, but I glimpsed no one who resembled my miniature. Would Robin have brought Mercy? I looked for a tiny woman, an elfin child, but the crowd kept shifting, and I couldn't spot them.

I paused at the bottom of the gangway, my bags arrayed at my feet, and watched the joyful reunions around me. Robin had obviously been detained. She had probably missed the train from London. Sooner or later she would appear; I had only to wait. But where? Not here on the dock, besieged by zealous porters. I was peering through the throng, searching for a lounge, when a man materialized in front of me.

"Miss Hamilton?"

"Yes?" My voice was shrill with relief.

"Giles Chapman, Miss Hamilton." He extended one bony hand. "Mr. Leighton's solicitor."

I took his hand, observing that Uncle Henry's lawyer looked the part. Giles Chapman was perhaps ten years older and three inches shorter than I. He was painfully thin and cadaverously pale, with thinning brown hair and watery blue eyes, which blinked at me through rimless spectacles.

"I've come to escort you to London," he said gratuitously. "Mr. Leighton notified me only this morning, and I was dreadfully worried I wouldn't know you. But I had no trouble picking you out. I must say you bear a keen resemblance to your sister."

"Who, I presume, is waiting for us in London."

"Umm." Giles Chapman cleared his throat. "Umm. Not exactly."

"Oh? Then where is Robin?"

"Umm. I wish I could say." He stared at his shoes, then lifted his weak blue eyes to mine. "I wish I could say. The fact is, Miss Hamilton, your sister has disappeared."

TWO

I woke not knowing where I was and sat up in the four-poster bed. There was a window at my right, and fuzzy slivers of light crept around the drapes, faintly illumining the room. A massive wardrobe loomed directly in front of me, flanked by a chest of drawers on one side and a dressing table on the other. This was not my sunny bedroom; had we moved again? Had Clara prevailed on Mr. Parker for larger, more elaborate quarters?

I shook my head, and my mind cleared. I was in Uncle Henry's London mansion, and Clara and Mr. Parker were in Chicago, thousands of miles behind me. I walked to the window and peered through the drapes, but if I anticipated a reassuring view of the Tower, I was doomed to disappointment. There was a miniature forest outside, and beyond that the merest glimpse of a neighboring house. The sky was gray, and a steady drizzle bathed the leaves of the trees.

I opened the drapes and crossed back toward the bed. A fireplace stood opposite the window. The clock on the mantel read nine. I had not yet been summoned to breakfast, and I perched on the edge of the bed, reviewing the events of the previous day.

Following his startling announcement, Giles Chapman had hustled me to the boat train, eluding my breathless questions:

"We shall have to hurry, Miss Hamilton. We'll discuss it on the train. Though I fear you'll find me sadly uninformed. I know nothing of your sister's activities, nothing at all."

Nor did he. After we were seated in the first-class carriage, Mr. Chapman unburdened himself, so to speak, and his report proved sketchy indeed.

Robin had left London "some time ago."

"How long ago, Mr. Chapman? Last week? Last month?"

"I really couldn't say."

"Where did she go?"

"I wasn't told."

"When was she due back?"

"I haven't any idea."

"Then how can you possibly say she has disappeared?"

"*I* did not," he replied stiffly. "Mr.

Leighton sent a note round this morning. He said you were expected in Southampton later in the day and that Mrs. Ashworth, who had intended to meet you, was missing. Yes – I beg your pardon – Mr. Leighton's word was 'missing.' "

It had taken me upwards of fifteen minutes to extract even these scraps of information; Giles Chapman was something less than a sparkling raconteur. I abandoned hope of further enlightenment and sat back. Mr. Chapman had no doubt conveyed, if unwittingly, a highly inaccurate representation of the situation. Robin had probably treated herself to a holiday and failed to return on schedule. Uncle Henry – that "persnickety merchant," as Father had called him – had peevishly pronounced her "missing." Robin's absence was by no means sinister. But why had she planned a journey on the very eve of my arrival?

We proceeded to London in silence, and at Waterloo Station Mr. Chapman hired a growler for the drive to Uncle Henry's house in St. James's Street. We found the house ablaze with electric lights, an innovation exceeding even Mr. Parker's imagination. The footman who answered our ring informed us, "Mr. and Mrs. Leighton have retired," and instructed a maid to show me to my room.

"Would you be wanting your bags unpacked?" she asked with an Irish lilt.

Would I? I had fulfilled my promise; I had come back to England. And what was I to do next?

"Not – not tonight," I stammered.

"Good night then, miss."

"Good night."

I undressed in the harsh, unfamiliar glare of electricity, extinguished the light, and crawled into bed. Apparently, Aunt Jane was not unduly concerned about Robin, I reflected. Nor wildly eager to receive me. It was not yet ten, and she had "retired" . . .

Oh, Father, what have you done to me? I'm a stranger here – alone, unwelcome . . . A black cloud of homesickness hovered over me, descended, descended, and I tumbled into sleep.

I felt a swelling lump in my throat and sternly reminded myself that self-pity was a barren emotion. I glanced around the room and, seeing no washstand, donned my dressing gown and ventured into the corridor. I located a bathroom at the end of the hall and bathed, then returned to my room and examined my limited wardrobe with a frown. I must tell Aunt Jane of Father's death, I recalled; perhaps the black would be most suitable. I

35

was pinning the last stubborn strands of hair in place when a maid tapped on the door and announced that breakfast "awaited my pleasure" in the dining room.

The maid, who said her name was Annie, led me through a maze of corridors and staircases to the entry hall. We passed the drawing room, the conservatory, the music room, and eventually reached the dining-room archway.

"Miss Hamilton, mum," Annie murmured and slipped away.

Aunt Jane had not, in fact, "awaited my pleasure." Her plate was nearly empty, and as she looked up, she emitted a satisfied belch. I stood on the threshold, staring at her quite rudely, I'm afraid, and attempted to mask my shock.

I had remembered Aunt Jane as a feminine version of Father: tall and slender, with dark-brown hair and piercing blue eyes. Evidently, Trade had proved an excellent provider. Her cheeks had ballooned to fleshy pouches, and her chin had multiplied alarmingly. Her arms rippled beneath sleeves that were altogether too snug, and her bosom strained the seams of her bodice. Only her coloring had aged like Father's: her hair was white, her eyes the faded blue of his.

"Well, does the cat have your tongue?"

Aunt Jane demanded irritably.

"I – I'm sorry. It's good to see you again, Aunt Jane."

"Yes. Thank God you have arrived. Please serve yourself." She tossed her head toward the tall mahogany sideboard behind her and began slathering butter on a scone. "I shan't mince words. Your uncle and I are most annoyed with Robin. After all we have done for her . . ."

I went to the sideboard and filled a plate with bacon, eggs, and a scone, gingerly avoiding the simmering kidneys. I poured a cup of coffee and took the chair across from Aunt Jane, whose fretful discourse had continued unabated.

". . . I am appalled by Robin's utter disregard of her responsibilities." She spoke through a shower of crumbs. "Appalled. I cannot imagine what she was thinking of –"

"Father died just over a month ago," I interrupted quietly.

"Oh?" She spooned a dollop of marmalade on her scone. "I am sorry to hear that. I had thought to write John of Robin's disgraceful behavior." She popped the scone in her mouth.

So much for mourning. I pushed my plate aside and laid down my fork.

"Where is Robin?" I asked wearily.

"If I knew that, I shouldn't be worrying myself half to death in her absence." Aunt Jane broke another scone; evidently her deep anxiety had not dulled her appetite. "I should send after her at once."

"She didn't tell you where she was going then," I said gratuitously.

"Indeed she did not."

"I suppose she felt she needed to get away for a day or two."

"A day or two was exactly what she proposed." Aunt Jane glared at the silver candelabrum in the middle of the table, as though it were Robin. "However, your sister has now been gone for a week."

"A week." Hardly a disappearance. "A week isn't so very long. Robin has had a difficult time of it –"

"That she has." Aunt Jane's expression softened almost imperceptibly. "Justin could not have been an easy man to live with. I daresay Robin was rather relieved when he – well, the Lord works in mysterious ways," she concluded piously.

"Yes, He does." I took shameless advantage of her moderating mood. "Nevertheless, Robin deserved a holiday, and I shouldn't have wanted her to cut it short on my account. A long rest will benefit both of them –"

"Both of them?" Aunt Jane echoed sharply.

"Robin and Mercy."

"Mercy! But that is the problem, Linnet: Mercy is here."

"Here?"

"Yes, in the room next to yours. I'm surprised you didn't hear her; she sobs and sniffles half the night –"

"Perhaps you should start at the beginning, Aunt Jane."

"It seems I must." A martyred sigh. "Robin left London precisely a week ago . . ."

Robin had brought Mercy to the house in St. James's Street early on that Tuesday morning, "totally without warning." She had advised Aunt Jane that she had "pressing business" outside London and would be away for "a few days." She would "certainly" return "before the weekend." Aunt Jane had graciously consented to care for Mercy and had, furthermore, appointed her *"chief coachman"* to drive Robin to Waterloo Station. Robin had not been seen or heard from since.

"I can only assume," Aunt Jane concluded, "that Robin has – that Robin – that there is a gentleman." She lowered her eyes, horrified by her own boldness.

A lover? ("I have been glancing over my journal and am most distressed.") A secret liaison, rationalized for months,

39

years; widowhood; a perusal of the journal; a sudden surge of guilt . . . It was, I admitted, a possibility.

"Have you questioned Mercy?" I asked.

"Mercy?" Aunt Jane swallowed a final morsel of scone and sniffed. "The child is only seven."

"But she might remember something."

"Oh, very well."

Aunt Jane tinkled the silver bell at her right hand, and yet another maid answered her summons. They conversed for a moment in whispers, and I studied my plate, weighing the dubious merits of cold eggs versus a cold scone. I elected the latter and had nearly finished it when the maid reappeared, fairly dragging a child in her wake.

"Good morning, Mercy, dear." Aunt Jane's warmth was patently artificial. "Come in, child. This is your Aunt Linnet."

Mercy bobbed her head but remained in the archway, assessing me with grave dark eyes. She was a tiny child, short for her age, I thought, and painfully thin. Her hair and eyes were black – Justin, I recalled, had been very dark – but her pointed face was fair like Robin's. I crossed the room, stooped, and embraced her awkwardly. She stood stiff and unyielding in my arms, and I entertained an angry suspicion that Aunt Jane had frightened

40

her out of her wits.

"I am so pleased to meet you at last, Mercy," I said, releasing her. "Your mother has told me a great deal about you, and I'm sure we shall become great friends."

"Have you come to find Mama?" she asked.

"Certainly not," I said cheerfully, "for your mama isn't lost. I can't find someone who isn't lost, now can I? If you think about it, I expect you'll remember just where she went."

"I *have* thought about it," she said, sounding strangely adult. "I don't know where she went."

"Then why don't you tell me what she said. Exactly what she said when she left."

"She said she had to pay a visit."

"A visit where?"

"To the country."

"Where in the country?"

"I don't know."

Her voice was flat, her face lifeless, and I wondered if she had always been this way or if Aunt Jane had made her the dark little puppet she was.

"Did she mention who it was she planned to visit?"

"No, ma'am."

"Well, I imagine your mama has many

41

friends. People who call at your house."

"No, ma'am."

"No? No one?"

"No, ma'am. Papa didn't care much for visitors."

"What about the gentleman? Isn't there a gentleman? A special friend of your mama's? Someone who brings you presents perhaps?"

"No, ma'am."

"This is obviously a waste of time," Aunt Jane interjected impatiently. "You are excused, Mercy. You and Victoria may lunch in the dining room today in honor of Aunt Linnet's arrival. That will be all."

Mercy bobbed her head again, a disturbingly mechanical gesture, and left the room.

"Who is Victoria ?" I asked.

"Mercy's doll. And apparently her only friend. Justin –" She heaved another sigh.

"Well." I resumed my seat and picked idly at the crumbs of my scone. "It seems we shall simply have to wait for Robin –"

"That, I fear, is impossible."

"Impossible? What do you mean?"

"I cannot accommodate Mercy indefinitely; I haven't the staff. You will have to make other arrangements, Linnet."

"I?" I gaped at her.

"You *are* her nearest relative."

"But surely Robin will return in a day or two, a week –"

"Surely? Your confidence far surpasses mine. I suspect your sister is quite enjoying her immoral adventure, and I do not intend to abet her sinful enterprise by keeping her child. You will have to make other arrangements," she repeated primly.

"I have no money, Aunt Jane." It was almost true; Father's bequest had been reduced to less than $100. "I've no place to go; I know no one else in England –"

"Then I would suggest you take Mercy to Justin's family."

"The Ashworths?"

"Yes. Ashwood isn't far from London. Your uncle and I traveled down for a wedding once. The elder son. His name escapes me."

"Edward."

"Yes, Edward."

"He died recently."

"I believe Robin mentioned that. I was sorry to hear it."

Aunt Jane fussed with a button on her bodice, and I suppressed an urge to fly across the table and wrap my hands around her fleshy throat. She was prepared to throw a defenseless child literally into the street – would unless I could locate Robin . . .

The journal. Perhaps there was a clue in the journal.

"Give me a little time, Aunt Jane," I pleaded. A chance to look round Robin's house. I'll go this afternoon –"

"I shall need the carriage this afternoon." She had managed to twist the button off her dress and lifted her pale-blue eyes to mine. "Douglas can drive you over tomorrow." A generous concession indeed. "If you are unable to establish Robin's whereabouts, you will take Mercy to Ashwood. Is that clear?"

"Very clear."

Aunt Jane flashed a triumphant smile and lustily rang her little bell for seconds.

Douglas (I had not determined whether this was his Christian or his surname) brought the horse to a halt and came around to assist me out of the brougham. I paused beside the carriage, gazing at the house. It was quite ordinary – a three-story yellow-brick with stucco dressings, the front door painted brown.

"I shan't be long, Douglas."

"Yes, miss."

He jammed a half-smoked cigar in his mouth and slouched against the brougham, and I approached the door. Robin had left Aunt Jane a key, which Aunt Jane had relayed to me. She had warned, however, that "there might be servants about," and I rang the bell.

"Yes?" She was plump, and her faded red hair and multitudinous freckles bespoke an Irish background. "Why, sure, and you must be Mrs. Ashworth's sister. She has spoken of you many times, she has. I'm Mrs. McDonald, Mrs. Ashworth's housekeeper."

"Miss Hamilton," I murmured.

"Miss Hamilton, of course. And happy I am to see you. I've been worried silly about Mrs. Ashworth. I trust she had a nice little outing?"

"I'm afraid I couldn't say, Mrs. McDonald. Robin – Mrs. Ashworth has not yet returned."

"Umm." Her pale-red eyebrows met in a frown.

"I had hoped you might shed some light on her – outing. Did she give no indication where she was going?"

"None. Though I must say the poor woman was overdue for a holiday. She's been terribly distraught."

"Since Dr. Ashworth's death, you mean."

"No, she took the doctor's passing very well actually. It was some weeks later –" She suffered a belated attack of discretion, and her voice trailed off.

"I understand there were problems in the marriage," I said conspiratorially.

"There are problems in every marriage."

"But in this one more than most?"

"Well, Dr. Ashworth was away a good deal. He came home at all hours of the night, covered with blood from his ghastly operations –" Mrs. McDonald shuddered. "But what am I thinking of? Come in, Miss Hamilton. Would you be wanting a cup of tea?"

"I think not." I stepped into the linoleum entrance hall. "My carriage is waiting." The words tripped glibly off my tongue, and I briefly pondered their irony. The Coachman's Daughter had a carriage waiting . . . "Then Mrs. Ashworth didn't even hint at her destination?"

"She did say she was going to the country, but beyond that –" Mrs. McDonald shook her head. "She's such a considerate woman, she is. My daughter – Maureen, my youngest – just birthed a fine baby boy. My fourteenth grandchild," she beamed. "But Maureen's first, and she had a nasty time of it. So when Mrs. Ashworth told me she'd be in the country for a few days, she suggested I go over to Maureen's and help her out. She said she could leave Miss Mercy with her aunt. She instructed me to be back on Saturday. Well, I came back, and there was no sign of Mrs. Ashworth or Miss Mercy. I've

46

been beside myself, I have."

"Oh, I doubt there's cause for alarm." I hesitated. I needed information, but I didn't wish to paint an unduly provocative picture of Robin's absence. "I expect she went off with a friend," I said.

"A friend?"

"Yes. I believe there's a gentleman." Her freckled face remained impassive. "An associate of Dr. Ashworth?" I prodded.

"I don't know how you got that idea." She shook her head again. "They didn't entertain, and Dr. Ashworth never brought home an associate that I remember. Dr. Ashworth favored his privacy, he did."

"I see." An impasse. "I'd like to look around if you don't mind."

"Mind? No indeed. Are you sure you wouldn't care for tea? Perhaps some lemonade?"

"No, thank you. Really, I shan't keep you."

I peered desultorily into the drawing room, which was situated to my right off the entry hall. I sensed Mrs. McDonald's curious green eyes on my back, and I stepped inside and idly fingered a vase. Discreet or no, I did not want her to know what I was searching for. She followed me to the dining room, where I poked at the silver serving pieces on the sideboard, and then to the library. I spotted a glass-fronted cabinet, filled with books, and my heart bounded.

"I believe I *would* like some tea," I said. "Lemon, no milk. I shall meet you back in the drawing room."

"Yes, miss." Her voice sagged with disappointment, but she left me, and I heard her footsteps tapping down the stairs to the kitchen.

I hurried across the library and opened the cabinet. There was an abundance of medical texts within – enormous tomes with indecipherable titles – and, on the bottom shelf, a row of thin, leather-bound volumes. I recognized the first of them as the red-covered journal Robin had started at thirteen, and I reached impatiently for the last. I opened it to the middle and began to read.

"Mrs. McDonald's second daughter (or is it her third?) is expecting again..." I flipped a dozen pages ahead. "I wonder if Mercy is old enough for piano instruction. She seems to have quite an ear for music..." A dozen pages more. "The piano lessons have not proved satisfactory. Miss Semple recommends I wait a year or two..." I turned to the final entry. "Justin does not find it becoming, and I must say I agree with him. I shall have to have another dress made, and the occasion is almost upon us."

I closed the book and stared at the blue cover. Was this what had "distressed" Robin? Mrs. McDonald's numerous grandchildren? Mercy's lack of musical talent? A gown Justin had disapproved? I replaced the slender volume on the shelf and recalled a habit of Robin's. She had kept her journal in the bedroom we shared, vowing to write in it "every single night."

The staircase lay at the end of the hall, and I paused at the bottom, cocking an ear for Mrs. McDonald. There was a faint clatter of dishes from the kitchen below, and I ascended the stairs.

A narrow, gloomy corridor bisected the second floor, and Mercy's room was located to the left, just at the top of the stairs. It was small and cheerful, with a yellow counterpane on the diminutive bed and frilly yellow curtains at the single window. Cheerful, but too neat – the counterpane smooth, the chest of drawers uncluttered, the yellow-painted toy-box closed. I felt a stir of empathy for the dark, solemn child I scarcely knew.

There was a water closet next and beyond that the master bedroom. It, too, was small and crammed with furniture: a brass bedstead, a bedside cabinet, a washstand, a rather dilapidated wardrobe, a dressing table with matching bench.

The bedside cabinet yielded an oil lamp and two magazines – medical publications nearly a year old. I went to the dressing table and found Robin's journal in the drawer, floating on a sea of scattered hairpins. The slender book was bound in gold, and I opened it to the front.

". . . my unspeakable suspicions possibly be true? And if they are, what must I do? Does my knowledge (or conjecture) bear upon the other problem? Do I possess a weapon or only a lingering echo of horror?"

There was no more. I leafed through the pages unbelievingly, but they were uniformly crisp and blank.

I checked the date at the top of the page: "May 11, 1890 (cont)." Continued from where? From one of the volumes in the library?

I descended the stairs and detected a clink of silverware in the drawing room. I crept back into the library and again opened the book-cabinet. I retrieved the blue volume, turned to the last page, and read the date: "Sept. 18, 1888." Perhaps they were out of order. I removed the dainty books one by one, but they were perfectly sequenced, from the first adolescent entry for April 4, 1875, to the final lament for the unacceptable dress.

One of Robin's journals was missing, I reflected, closing the cabinet. Had she taken it with her? If so, why? If not, where was it; had it been stolen or hidden or destroyed? There was a rustle behind me, and I whirled around to meet Mrs. McDonald's quizzical green eyes.

"I –" But a flimsy fabrication would not do. "I am ready for my tea now," I said haughtily, every inch the Gentlewoman.

The teacup was chipped, and it set me to wondering about Robin's financial situation. I glanced up at Mrs. McDonald, who hovered attentively at my elbow.

"Are there other servants?" I asked.

"There were."

"And they have been discharged?"

"She. Katie, the maid. Two months since. I'm afraid Mrs. Ashworth –" A calculated sigh.

"And what of yourself, Mrs. McDonald?"

"I have been paid through the end of the month."

The end of the month. Ten days away. I could bring Mercy to the house in Spring Street ... I shook my head. It would be too cruel – to deposit her in these familiar surroundings, only, perhaps, to spirit her off again less than a fortnight hence.

"I beg your pardon?" Mrs. McDonald

51

jarred me from my reverie.

"Nothing." I swallowed the dregs of my tea, which was altogether too weak. "I really must be going. I am confident Mrs. Ashworth will return to London very shortly. If not – if not, I shall be in touch with you about your position."

"Yes, miss."

She trailed me to the door, her lips fairly quivering with a flood of unasked questions. I paused with my hand on the tarnished brass knob.

"If you hear from Mrs. Ashworth, please advise her that I have gone to Ashwood."

"To Ashwood? To Dr. Ashworth's people?" Her expression was one of ill-concealed astonishment.

"Yes. Is that so unusual?"

"I – I suppose not," she stammered. "I had the impression –" She stopped.

"What impression?"

"That –" She chose her words with care. "That Mrs. Ashworth did not believe herself welcome at Ashwood."

"I am not Mrs. Ashworth," I said tartly. "Good day."

I felt her eyes upon me as I bustled toward the brougham, and I silently apologized for my sharpness. In fact, she had caught me unawares. Robin not welcome at Ashwood?

Why? And what sort of welcome awaited me, a stranger?

Douglas and I got enmeshed in one of London's beastly traffic jams, and while he cursed – loudly and imaginatively – I pondered Robin's odd behavior.

She had been, like Mercy, a solemn child, responsible to a fault; how could she have changed so radically? Love, I gathered, wreaked amazing transformations, so perhaps Love *had* enticed her into an "immoral adventure." But how had she managed to conduct an affair without arousing Mrs. McDonald's lively suspicions? Or had the shrewd housekeeper deceived me? I thought not. And why had Robin taken her journal, if indeed she had? Further to thwart Mrs. McDonald's prying eyes?

Her journal: "...unspeakable suspicions..." Of whom or what? Had Robin been widowed only to find evidence that her lover was married? What was "the other problem"? Her finances? Then how did the former "bear upon" the latter? Robin believed her "conjecture" might prove a "weapon," which suggested extortion. Yet she and her lover had apparently gone on holiday together ...

"...A lingering echo of horror." I had no

experience of love, but I had never heard it described as horrible. Doomed, yes, dangerous, even degrading; not horrible. So had Robin spoken of love on that last page of her journal or of something else entirely?

It was nearly dinner time when we reached the house in St. James's Street, and Uncle Henry, his stomach audibly rumbling, was pacing the entry hall in front of the dining-room archway. He had been in Birmingham the evening before, and now he greeted me with relative warmth, planting a dry kiss on my forehead. I stepped back, my hand still resting in his huge paw, and studied him.

The years had marked him as well, I observed. He was portly – though not so stout as Aunt Jane – and his flowing red beard had given way to an enormous, pinkish mustache and equally luxuriant side whiskers. This profusion of facial hair contrasted dramatically with his gleaming scalp, which was as bald as the proverbial egg.

We exchanged pleasantries. Uncle Henry condoled with me ("John" – in death – "was a splendid fellow"), and I inquired politely after his far-flung business enterprises. We were groping for a new topic when Aunt Jane appeared and led us into the dining room.

"Were you able to locate Robin?" she asked halfway through the soup.

"No. No, I wasn't."

"The servants were out?"

"No, I spoke with Mrs. McDonald, Robin's housekeeper. But she's as much in the dark as we."

"Well, that settles the matter then, doesn't it?"

She smacked her lips, and I couldn't determine whether she was perversely pleased or simply appreciative of the mulligatawny.

I turned to Uncle Henry. "Mrs. McDonald implied that Robin has been in rather straitened circumstances."

"I shouldn't be surprised."

He frowned at Aunt Jane, who obediently rang her silver bell. The empty soup bowls were whisked away, to be supplanted by juicy slabs of roast beef and tiny boiled potatoes. Uncle Henry attacked his beef with relish.

"Justin didn't leave her well fixed?" I said, toying with a potato.

"I suppose not. I believe it takes considerable time for a physician to establish a lucrative practice."

"Are the Ashworths assisting her? Financially, I mean?"

"I'm sure I wouldn't know." Like most wealthy men, Uncle Henry disdained the vulgar discussion of money.

"Does she get on with them? The

Ashworths? Mrs. McDonald indicated there might be a rift."

"Your Mrs. McDonald sounds too presumptuous by half. I don't think Justin was especially close to his family, but a rift?" He drowned the suggestion with a generous swallow of red wine. "I shall telegraph down to Ashwood tomorrow and tell them to expect you on Friday."

"But what if there *is* a feud of some sort?" I pressed. "Lady Margaret might well refuse to receive us."

"Umm." He glowered at a slice of bread.

"It would be better by far if we stayed here –"

"A note." Uncle Henry snapped his fingers. "Yes, a note. If we post it tomorrow, it will arrive on Friday. We shall put you on an afternoon train, and they'll have several hours' notice of your arrival, no more –"

He warmed to his calculations, and I sighed. Mercy and I, it seemed, were destined to go to Ashwood.

THREE

The journey from London could not have been a long one; Leatherhead was but twenty miles from the city. It seemed, however, interminable, for Mercy emerged from her shell to batter me with questions.

Where was her mama?

"I don't know, dear, but I'm certain she'll be back very soon."

"How long shall we stay at Ashwood?"

"Only until your mama returns to London."

"And when will that be?"

"Very soon," I repeated patiently.

"If you don't know where she is, how do you know when she'll come home?"

An excellent point and one I elected to parry. "Why don't you tell me about Ashwood. Is it a lovely place?"

"I don't remember."

"Oh? You don't visit often then?"

"If I did, I *would* remember, wouldn't I?" She straightened Victoria's skirts rather huffily. "Mama says they took me there when I was a baby. She and Papa."

"I see." Was Mercy not welcome at

Ashwood either? "Well, we shall both have a great adventure then, shan't we?"

"Umm. What was it like in America? Were you ever attacked by Indians?"

"Indeed not. I lived in a most civilized place. Almost as civilized as London."

I described the bustling city on Lake Michigan, Mr. Parker's turreted mansion, the great chestnut trotters, but Mercy soon grew restive. She turned away, plastered Victoria's porcelain nose to the window and began rattling off the sights as they fled by.

I extracted a handkerchief from the pocket of my skirt and dabbed at the fine film of perspiration that had formed on my brow. I had been neatly trapped, I reflected. Mrs. McDonald would direct Robin to Ashwood if Robin contacted the house in Spring Street. Aunt Jane would notify me if Robin got in touch with her. But I had no reason to hope – my assurances to Mercy notwithstanding – that Robin would turn up "very soon."

And until she did, Mercy was my responsibility. My responsibility, and I knew nothing, absolutely nothing, about children.

"Victoria wants to go home," Mercy whined.

"Well, you must tell Victoria that is quite impossible," I said firmly.

Mercy's lips quivered into a pout, and I

blotted my forehead again.

At last the train ground to a halt at the Leatherhead terminal. I dragged Mercy down the steps (she wished to "go on to France") and engaged a porter to retrieve our portmanteaux. His evil stare elicited an outrageous gratuity, and as he swaggered off, I gazed irritably around the station.

There were few travelers to Leatherhead on this late-May afternoon. Two men – commercial representatives, I surmised – strode briskly into the terminal. A boy paced nervously up and down the platform; I wondered if he had been expelled from school. Two men, a boy, Mercy, and I. I spotted a private carriage at one end of the station and watched it for several minutes. The boy continued his restless pacing, and the men had disappeared; it seemed worth an inquiry.

"I am going to speak to the driver," I said to Mercy, nodding over my shoulder. "Wait for me *right here*."

"Victoria wants to go to France."

"I'm afraid Victoria's desires far exceed her means. Tell Victoria to wait for me right here. Tell Victoria she will be in very serious trouble if she budges so much as a single inch."

I walked toward the carriage, turning once

to glower at my charges. I was gratified to note that Mercy's feet seemed rooted to the railway platform.

"Excuse me."

The man on the box was in his late twenties, I guessed, with pale-brown hair and absent gray eyes.

"Are you by chance from Ashwood?"

"Ashwood," he echoed dully. "Yes'm."

"Splendid. I am Miss Hamilton."

I might as well have announced that I was President Benjamin Harrison; he appeared totally bewildered.

"I believe they were expecting me? The Ashworths?"

Nothing.

"I wrote Lady Margaret . . ."

A dim glimmer of comprehension. "Lady Margaret. Yes'm. I'm Alf."

"Alf." He was obviously simple. "Well, Alf, I am the person you were sent to meet. I and the young lady." I gestured to Mercy, still paralyzed on the platform behind me. "If you could assist us with our bags . . ."

Alf was scarcely a model of efficiency, and it took him some ten minutes to arrange the luggage to his liking. He handed us awkwardly into the brougham, remounted the box, and clucked to the horse – a scrawny, ill-groomed bay. We traversed the main street of the town, and I idly observed a tailors' establishment, a bakery, an ancient hotel. We descended a steep hill, passed another inn, and clattered over an arched brick bridge. I did not know our direction nor what river we crossed, which reinforced my sense of helpless entrapment.

"Victoria is hot," Mercy said petulantly.

"So is Aunt Linnet," I snapped.

I estimated it to be about six miles from Leatherhead to Ashwood. In the intervening countryside we passed beech woods, well-tended fields of wheat and oats, and here and there a grazing herd of dairy cattle. Mercy described the scenery to Victoria in excruciating detail – "You see, there is a horse pulling a wagon, a red wagon. I can't tell whether the horse is black or brown; can you tell, Victoria? Never mind; look at the cows. I prefer the spotted ones, though the white ones are nice as well, aren't they?" – and by the time we entered the beech-lined drive of Ashwood, I had developed a pounding headache.

The drive was a long one – perhaps half a mile – and formed an irregular arc as it approached the house. I suppose I had imagined Ashwood to be similar to Hamilton Oaks, but it more nearly resembled Clara's depiction of Rosemont Plantation. It was severely rectangular and built of white brick, with chimneys thrusting symmetrically from the roof and columns guarding the porch.

Alf stopped directly in front of the porch, clambered down from the box, and sauntered up the low stairs to the front door. He knocked perfunctorily, then opened the door and stepped inside. Several minutes elapsed, and I feared he had forgotten his passengers altogether. I had begun to fumble with the door handle when Alf reappeared, followed by a middle-aged man. The latter was of medium height, slender, ramrod straight, and clad in impeccable black trousers and frock coat. He was clearly displeased – whether with Alf, with us, or with the dismal state of the world in general, I could not determine. He opened the carriage door and peered inside.

"Miss Hamilton." His tone suggested that he had hoped to find the brougham empty after all.

"Yes."

"I am Hines, Lady Margaret's butler." He assisted us out of the carriage – me first, then Mercy – and inspected us coolly. "I trust you had a pleasant trip?"

"Quite pleasant, thank you."

"Well."

His gray eyes flickered from us to the

brougham, as though recommending that we resume our places and depart at once. I smoothed my wrinkled blue skirt and studiedly avoided his gaze.

"Well," he said again. "Mrs. Abbott is waiting. Take the bags upstairs, Alf. Leave them in the corridor."

He turned and stalked up the shallow steps and through the open door. I took Mercy's hand – not certain whether I was imparting or seeking comfort – and followed.

I had envisioned Mrs. Abbott as a female Hines, but she proved a pleasant surprise. She was a short, stout woman with untidy gray hair and merry blue eyes. She rushed forward as we crossed the threshold, hands outstretched, black skirt rustling beneath a crisp white apron.

"And here they are," she twittered, seizing my hand in hers. "Welcome to Ashwood, Miss Hamilton. A beastly day for traveling, wasn't it? So very warm. The poor, dear lamb must be quite done in." This with a vigorous ruffling of Mercy's black hair. "I'll wager a glass of lemonade would hit the spot –"

"This is not the time for lemonade, Mrs. Abbott," Hines interjected icily. "The ladies must be shown to their rooms. Alice?" His eyes darted around the entry hall, into the drawing room on the right, into the library on the left. "Alice?"

"Alice is busy," Mrs. Abbott snapped. "I shall escort the ladies. Miss Hamilton? Miss Ashworth?"

She marched down the hall to the staircase, and I tugged Mercy after her.

"He is the most *domineering* man," Mrs. Abbott muttered, panting her way up the stairs. "The Prince of Wales himself, one would think. He credits me with no sense at all, but one of these days –" We had reached the second-floor corridor, and her threat expired in a wheeze. "Miss Ashworth – Miss Mercy, may I say? – is in here –"

It reminded me of Mercy's room in Spring Street, except that the color scheme was blue rather than yellow – blue curtains fluttering in the spring breeze, a blue counterpane, even a blue toy-box. Had Justin had a sister? I wondered. Odd that I didn't know.

"Would you care for a nap?" Mrs. Abbott guided Mercy deftly to the narrow bed. "Yes, you really must rest up. Your aunt will be just down the hall –"

Mrs. Abbott helped Mercy out of her dress, and the dark, frail child – reduced to chemise and petticoat – crawled into bed, cradling Victoria protectively to her bosom. "Just down the hall," Mrs. Abbott crooned, and

64

Mercy was asleep before we had closed her door behind us.

My own room was considerably less cheerful than Mercy's, with heavy, maroon-damask drapes, a matching counterpane, a profusion of dark, elaborately carved furniture. Mrs. Abbott bustled about, opening the drapes, smoothing the counterpane, attacking imaginary specks of dust with one corner of her white apron.

"There," she beamed at last. "I believe everything is in order. The water closet is next door, and dinner is at seven. Miss Mercy's dinner will be brought up, of course; I've instructed Alice . . ."

She chattered on, and my head, already throbbing, began to whirl with confusion.

"Pardon me, Mrs. Abbott." I interrupted her in mid-word. "I presume you are the housekeeper?"

"Yes and no. I was *engaged* as cook. But Ashwood is a trifle shorthanded at the moment, and someone had to take charge. Mr. Hines would drive the maids off in a day; he's that full of himself. Not that my wages are like to a housekeeper's; no, indeed." Mrs. Abbott's sigh underscored the monumental injustice of her situation. "So I spend most of my time in the kitchen. If you find yourself in need of refreshment, there's generally a treat –"

"Thank you. And who is Alice?"

"One of the housemaids. Not as responsible as one might wish, I'm sorry to say." She pursed her lips and dropped her voice. "I didn't wish to mention it to Mr. Hines, but Alice is nowhere to be found. Dallying with one of the stable boys, I daresay. Sooner or later, she will pay for her sinful ways; you mark my words. But, as I said, I've instructed Alice to watch after Miss Mercy, and if the wicked girl ever returns –"

"Mrs. Abbott!" Hines's voice reverberated down the corridor.

"You see?" she hissed. "His Royal Highness in the flesh. I'd best be getting along to the kitchen. If you want anything –"

"Mrs. Abbott!"

"In a moment, Mr. Hines!" she shrieked. "If you want anything, there's the bell." She indicated a frayed rope near the bed. "Did I say dinner is at seven?"

"Yes, Mrs. Abbott. Thank you."

She smiled, then sailed grimly through the door, leaving it ajar. I moved to close it and overheard a fragment of conversation.

"Alice will be free in due course," Mrs. Abbott said.

An indecipherable masculine mumble.

"Well, Lady Margaret has said nothing of the sort to me. And until she does, I intend to be civil."

There were heavy footsteps on the stairs, and I shut the door and leaned against it. Nothing of what sort? Was Miss Hamilton – like her sister and niece before her – not welcome at Ashwood?

There was a clock on the mantel here as well, and as its hands neared seven, I felt moderately better. I had unpacked my portmanteau, hanging my dresses in the wardrobe, consigning my underthings to the chest of drawers. I had freshened up as best I could; the water closet was just that – not a bathroom – and I gazed at the empty basin on the washstand and silently cursed "wicked" Alice. I left my dark, depressing bedroom and cracked Mercy's door. She was deep in conversation with a red-haired, black-clad figure whose face I couldn't see – the fabled Alice? I pulled the door silently to and descended the stairs.

Mrs. Abbott had not given me directions to the dining room, but it was not difficult to find. I recalled that the drawing room and library lay at the front of the house and the music room at the bottom of the stairs. The dining room, as I had expected, was situated across the entry hall from the latter.

Ashwood was not yet equipped with gas light, much less electricity, and the chandelier above the great oaken table winked with half a hundred candles. The table was set for four, and as I stepped into the room, a woman leaped from one of the side chairs.

"Miss Hamilton?" she said nervously.

"Yes."

"I am Caitlin Ashworth."

She came around the table but stopped several yards in front of me, her eyes riveted to some fascinating spectacle over my shoulder. She was about my age, I thought – perhaps two or three years older. She was not above five feet tall and thin to the verge of emaciation. Her hair was mouse-brown, as were her eyes, and she wore rimless spectacles, which persisted in sliding down her nose. She reminded me of someone, but I could not pinpoint the resemblance.

Caitlin Ashworth. Who was Caitlin Ashworth? I hazarded a guess.

"You must be Edward's –"

"Sister," she concluded breathlessly. I would have said "widow." "Justin's sister. I –" But she had exhausted her immediate store of words.

"Well, we are related then, aren't we?

68

If distantly." I spoke to her as I might have to Mercy, but there was something vulnerable, childlike about her. "I'm Robin's sister."

"I knew that. And would have, at any rate. You –"

She was interrupted by a swish of skirts and an affected peal of feminine laughter. Miss Ashworth and I turned together to find a strikingly handsome couple framed in the dining-room archway.

The woman (twenty-seven, thirty?) was tall and slender, with artfully arranged blond hair and glittering green eyes. Her gown, though black, was in no way modest: it had short, puffed sleeves and was slashed daringly low in the front. The creamy flesh it so generously exposed served as backdrop for a splendid collection of jewels – sparkling emeralds that perfectly matched her adamantine eyes.

Her companion was at least a head taller than she – six feet four or five, I estimated. He was as dark as she was fair, his hair and eyes nearly black, his skin burned brown by the sun. Evidently, he had not sought her sartorial guidance; he wore a casual tweed suit.

"Well, our guest has arrived safely, I see." The woman's tone, like Hines's earlier in the day, was one of ill-disguised disappointment.

"And has already made dear Caitlin's acquaintance, it appears. Perhaps you would do the honors, Caitlin?"

Caitlin Ashworth lowered her eyes, and I felt as though I were witnessing the baiting of a helpless animal.

"I am Linnet Hamilton," I said quietly.

"Miss Hamilton, of course." As if she had finally remembered our brief encounter at some scintillating gala. "I am Mrs. Ashworth. Mrs. Edward Ashworth. Mrs. Glynis Ashworth. And this" – she gestured possessively toward the man at her side, whose arm she still clung to – "is Mr. Carlisle."

"Sean Carlisle." He smiled, and I felt an odd tremor somewhere in my midsection.

"Dinner then?" Mrs. Ashworth's voice seemed a trifle shrill. "Shall we discover what new concoction Mrs. Abbott chooses to foist upon us tonight?"

Mrs. Abbott, in fact, presented a most commendable chicken curry with boiled rice and the appropriate condiments. Mrs. Ashworth occupied the head of the table, Mr. Carlisle the foot, and Caitlin Ashworth and I the sides. The conversation was incessant but not especially enlightening, as it consisted primarily of a monologue by Mrs. Glynis Ashworth. Everything in life, I learned, was "tiresome": the weather was tiresome; the current fashions were tiresome; the servants were tiresome. I suspected, though she did not say it, that widowhood was also tiresome.

I picked at my food and covertly studied Mr. Carlisle, who was quite the most attractive man I had ever met. What was his relationship to the Ashworths, I wondered, specifically to Mrs. Glynis? Was he, as Aunt Jane would have put it, "an admirer"? Surely not; she had been widowed for less than two months. At one point he mentioned having "reviewed the books" and "judged everything in order." A prospective buyer then? Did Mrs. Ashworth hope to be mistress of Ashwood twice over?

"Perhaps Miss Hamilton would spin us a few tales of her life in the United States," Mr. Carlisle said. We had been served coffee and a pudding Father would have adored. "It's a marvelous country, I'm told –"

"A tiresome one, I should say." Again that shrill undertone. "One political scandal after another; apparently the savages have seized control of the government . . ."

Perhaps I only wanted to believe that Mr. Carlisle flashed me an apologetic smile.

Dinner drew to a close, and we stood up. Glynis Ashworth suggested we adjourn to the music room, where, I gathered, she

71

would favor us with an impromptu concert. I was debating whether to plead exhaustion or a headache (both, unfortunately, legitimate excuses) when a maid tapped me discreetly on the arm.

"Mary, miss." She bobbed an abbreviated curtsy. "Lady Margaret will see you now."

As Mary led me through the dining room and the library and into a narrow corridor, I rehearsed my imminent chat with Lady Margaret. My note had been deliberately vague: I had introduced myself as "Robin's sister, recently returned from abroad," and had announced I was bringing Mercy to Ashwood for "a visit." I supposed Lady Margaret would pose any number of awkward questions.

Mary tapped on a door at the end of the hall and, responding to an acknowledgment I couldn't hear, opened it.

"Miss Hamilton, Lady Margaret."

She curtsied again, pulled me rather unceremoniously through the door, and closed it behind me.

Lady Margaret was ensconced in an old-fashioned curtained bed, two or three plump pillows arranged behind her. Her hair was white, her face waxen, her eyes – in shocking contrast – black. She bore clear evidence of the stroke Robin had reported: her right eye drooped permanently downward, and her mouth, on that side, was frozen in a chilly grin. A mauve dressing gown enhanced her cadaverous aspect.

"Miss Hamilton." Her voice was a surprise: deep, musical, harboring unmistakable traces of Scotland.

"Yes, ma'am?" I was, I must confess, intimidated.

"Please forgive my neglect. I am not, as I fear you see for yourself, in good health. Have not been in good health for some time. Then the deaths of my sons, coming one upon the other as they did –"

She paused, and I felt, perhaps, uncharitably, that the pause was intended to be maximally poignant.

"I was sorry to hear of your cruel losses," I murmured politely. "I was not acquainted with either of your sons –"

"Oh?" She sounded oddly relieved. "And how is dear Robin?"

I decided impulsively to dissemble. "I haven't seen my sister, Lady Margaret. I arrived in England only Monday, and Robin is traveling outside London."

"Traveling? How strange. I was under the impression she planned to return directly to the city."

It was a moment before I registered her

73

words. "Return from where?" I asked sharply.

"Why, from Ashwood, of course."

"Robin was *here?* And when was this?"

"Last week? Yes." She frowned, further distorting her ravaged face. "She arrived on the Tuesday and departed on the Thursday. Alf drove her to the station in Leatherhead, where she was to take the early train to London."

"And did she? Did she board the London train?"

"I couldn't say, Miss Hamilton. Nor, I suspect, could Alf. He is, as I'm sure you've observed, exceedingly slow." She hesitated. "Am I to assume you do not know your sister's whereabouts?"

"Yes. That is, I don't know where Robin is. Why did she come to Ashwood?" A tactless question perhaps.

"A courtesy call; nothing more. She was unable to attend Edward's funeral – ill, I believe. She wished to extend her condolences."

Did her reply ring false? I stared into her black eyes, but her terrible face was impassive.

"And why have *you* come to Ashwood, Miss Hamilton?" Her abrupt inquiry terminated my speculation.

"Only to escort Mercy," I said. "The child must stay here during Robin's absence."

"That is quite out of the question," Lady Margaret said flatly.

"Why?"

I believe she had anticipated instant capitulation, for she seemed confused and fumbled with the lace at her throat.

"The – the child is at a most difficult age. Yes. She would require constant care, a personal maid at the least, and we are indecently understaffed. We've no suitable amusements. No, it is out of the question," she repeated.

"I'm afraid there is no alternative, Lady Margaret."

"No alternative?" Her voice was shrill, like that of Mrs. Glynis. "Robin distinctly stated that Mercy was with her aunt, Mrs. Leighton, is it?"

"Yes, Mrs. Leighton. But Aunt Jane can't keep Mercy any longer. She lacks the staff," I added pointedly.

"Well, surely there are servants at Robin's home –"

"Only a housekeeper and only for another week."

"Another week? And why is that?"

I had, according to Father, inherited my mother's Irish temper, and I felt it snap.

"Because Robin left no money, Lady Margaret. Not a farthing, as you would say. And I haven't – to use the American expression – a dime to my name. I am utterly incapable of maintaining Robin's household. Do you wish me to take Mercy to an orphanage? Or maybe she might seek employment in a match factory –"

"Miss Hamilton!"

I could not determine whether she was angry or merely startled, and I was too enraged to care.

"Miss Hamilton." Tired. "If it is a matter of money –"

"Yes?"

She shook her head. "Frankly, you have caught me unawares. I shall have to explore the possibilities. In the meantime –"

"In the meantime, Mercy and I shall remain at Ashwood." A brave pronouncement; I hoped she could not detect the tremor in my voice.

"Perhaps." Her lips, on the mobile side of her face, thinned. "We shall discuss it again shortly. Good evening, Miss Hamilton."

I retraced the route that Mary and I had taken, successfully skirting the music room, from which emanated an uninspired rendition of "Oh, Promise Me." I ascended the stairs and cautiously opened Mercy's door. Her room was dark, and her breathing floated softly, rhythmically, from the canopied bed. My responsibility; no one wanted her . . .

In my own room the oil lamp had been lit, and I collapsed on the bed and gazed into its dancing flame. Lady Margaret's revelation had muddied the waters considerably.

Robin, estranged from the Ashworths for half a dozen years, had suddenly ventured down to Surrey. To pay a "courtesy call"? I doubted it. It seemed more likely, to borrow another of Lady Margaret's phrases, that it was a "matter of money," that Robin had come to Ashwood seeking financial assistance and had been summarily dismissed. In which case, I had *not* caught Lady Margaret unawares, but perhaps I had probed a festering wound. Perhaps the Ashworths were themselves financially embarrassed, Ashwood "indecently understaffed" because Lady Margaret could no longer afford a full complement of servants. Perhaps Mercy represented another mouth which could not be fed, another body which could not be clothed.

And what of Robin? Sent from Ashwood empty-handed, she had evidently carried her search elsewhere – to a friend, a distant relative, her lover . . . Her lover. Why, if I had correctly interpreted her journal, had she not drawn her "weapon" in the beginning, not approached him at the start?

There was an almost inaudible tap at the door, and I opened it to Caitlin Ashworth, visibly trembling in the corridor.

"Come in, Miss Ashworth."

"Are you certain?" I was soon to learn that she invariably spoke in this tremulous whisper. "I know you must be dreadfully tired –"

"No, please do come in."

She stepped timidly across the threshold; I was scarcely able to close the door behind her limp brown skirt. Once inside, she lost her tenuous courage and stared resolutely at the bare floor.

I am not endowed with any remarkable degree of patience, but Caitlin Ashworth – despite the fact that she was several years my senior – stirred some latent maternal instinct within me.

"I may be here for some time," I said kindly, as the silence grew oppressive. "I do hope we shall be friends. If you would call me Linnet, I should like to call you Caitlin."

She nodded eagerly, then embarked upon a painstaking examination of the Turkish carpet beside the bed. There was another protracted silence.

"Well, I thought dinner excellent, didn't

you?" I said brightly.

"Umm."

"A treat for me especially. Indian food is not yet popular in the United States. No, my father's employer" – did Caitlin know I was a Coachman's Daughter? – "had interests in the meat-packing industry, and we generally ate beef. Mr. Parker favored sirloin steak in particular –" I suspected I could narrate the entire history of my life without a single syllable of response. I changed the subject. "Who is Mr. Carlisle?" I asked, with studied nonchalance.

"My cousin."

"Your cousin."

"Uncle Angus's son."

"Uncle Angus?"

"Mother's brother."

"I see. He's some years older than you, I assume? Mr. Carlisle?"

"Sean is thirty-three. He and Justin were born on the same day."

"They must have been great friends then."

"Yes."

"Has Mr. Carlisle been at Ashwood long?"

"Upwards of a month."

"How nice. I'm sure his presence is a comfort."

"More than that. He took over the estate when Edward –" Her voice trailed off.

79

The estate and Edward's wife as well? "Apparently he and Mrs. Ashworth are – friends."

"Well, Glynis would have it so, wouldn't she?" Caitlin, relatively speaking, erupted with passion. "But I don't think she will find Sean as – as tractable as my brother was." She directed her attention to the flickering light on the bedside cabinet.

Was it Robin she reminded me of? Tiny, shy Robin?

"I understand my sister was here recently," I said.

"Yes. I started to mention it before: you look just like her." Caitlin's eyes brushed mine, then fled to the safety of the wardrobe.

"Did you talk with her at any length?" I asked.

"No."

"I thought she might have mentioned a problem of some sort. A specific reason for coming to Ashwood."

"No." Caitlin hesitated. "You haven't seen her then? Haven't heard from her?"

"No, I believe she's visiting friends."

Caitlin gazed at the hem of her skirt, at the chest of drawers, back at me. "You must leave Ashwood, Linnet," she said at last, her voice uncharacteristically firm. "At once. Tomorrow. On the first train if possible."

"And why is that?" I said mildly.

"You're in danger here."

"What kind of danger?"

"I don't know!" Her eyes darted frantically about the room. "I can't say! Just go; go before it's too late –"

She flung open the door and stumbled into the hall, tripping over her skirt, which was half an inch too long. The door crashed shut behind her, and I frowned at it.

Danger? Or had Lady Margaret begun to marshal her forces?

FOUR

"La, la, la. La, da, da."

If I must dream of music, I thought, could I not devise something more soothing than this off-key humming?

"La, la, la." Splash, splash. "La, da, da. Good morning, Miss Hamilton." I opened one eye and found a smiling, freckled face hovering just over mine. "Alice, miss. I hate to wake you, but we breakfast early in the country, we do."

I struggled upright and looked at the clock. Seven. Early indeed.

"There's hot water in the basin."

And about time, I thought irritably.

"I lit your lamp last evening," she said defensively, as though reading my mind. "Evidently you hadn't got back from dinner yet."

"Evidently not." I tended to be grouchy early in the morning.

"Will there be anything else, miss?"

She was red-haired and green-eyed; she might have been one of Mrs. McDonald's myriad daughters. She wore a skimpy black dress that artfully exhibited her voluptuous curves; plumpness would come in time. Her eyes sparkled with curiosity, and I suspected she knew a good deal about my brief stay at Ashwood.

"Actually, I didn't return directly from dinner," I said, testing my theory. "I went to see Lady Margaret."

"So I understand. It's none of my concern, of course, but I hope you won't be too hard on her. The poor woman has had a terrible siege of bad luck, she has. She nearly died from her stroke, and then for her sons to go like that –" Alice snapped her fingers. "One doesn't wonder she's snippy. Though I can understand your sister being put out; Lady Margaret gave *her* short shrift, that's for certain."

"They quarreled then? Lady Margaret and Mrs. Ashworth?"

"I should say so. But then your sister would have told you about it, wouldn't she?"

Apparently, Mary's eavesdropping had not proved wholly successful. "I haven't spoken with my sister since she left Ashwood."

"Oh. Oh, I see. Well, far be it from me –" She lowered her eyes.

(*It is most unseemly to gossip with the servants.* Yes, Father, but are the Ashworths likely to enlighten me?)

"I was afraid there would be an argument." I managed a credible sigh. "Robin's errand was a – a delicate one. If you could tell me exactly what occurred –"

She needed no prodding. "Well, Mrs. Ashworth arrived on a Tuesday, late morning, as I recall. To begin with, Lady Margaret kept her cooling her heels the entire day. Not that I blame Lady Margaret," she added hurriedly. "The poor woman tires very easily. At any rate, it was well after dinner when your sister was summoned to Lady Margaret's room. Naturally, I have no way of knowing what might have been said" – Alice pursed her ripe lips – "but the upshot was Mrs. Ashworth insisted on a tour of the estate. So Mr. Carlisle took her out –"

"Mr. Carlisle did?"

83

"Yes. Early the next afternoon. I didn't see Mrs. Ashworth come back, but Mrs. Abbott said she was dreadfully upset. And I know for a fact she refused dinner; I brought up a tray, and Mrs. Ashworth sent me away. Shortly after that she went to Lady Margaret again, and they had a fearful row. Mary said Mrs. Ashworth looked a very ghost when she left Lady Margaret's room."

"And Robin departed the following morning."

Alice nodded. "Just after dawn. I was dressing and happened to look out the window as she got in the carriage. Then they drove off –"

"She and Alf?"

"Yes, Alf was on the box. They drove off, and that was that."

Interesting. I revised the scenario I had composed the night before, casting Sean Carlisle in the villain's role. First evening: Lady Margaret sees Robin, explains that Mr. Carlisle is now in charge of Ashwood. Robin requests an audience with Mr. Carlisle, that is, a tour of the estate. Second day: The audience is eminently unsatisfactory; Mr. Carlisle refuses Robin's plea for money and upsets her "dreadfully." Second evening: Robin goes back to Lady Margaret, and there is a heated discussion. Robin demands assistance; Lady

84

Margaret reiterates Mr. Carlisle's position. Interesting.

"Did Robin visit often?" I asked aloud.

"I'm sure I couldn't say, miss. I've been at Ashwood only a month or so myself. I came just after the fire, just after Dr. Ashworth's death. A sad time, that. And then when Mr. Ashworth passed as well –" She shook her head. "Now that I think on it, all the servants are new. All except Mr. Hines and his son, Alf."

"Alf is Hines's son?"

"Yes. Hard to figure, isn't it? They say Mrs. Hines was a clever woman; she was housekeeper here many years ago. But she died when Alf was born. A very difficult birth; maybe Alf's brain got rattled in the process." She shook her head again. "Fortunately, Mr. Hines has another son. The tenant at Long Hill Farm. A splendid-*looking* man, I can tell you." There was a salacious gleam in Alice's green eyes.

"What happened to the servants? The ones who were here before? Were they discharged?"

"I don't know. I *suspect* –" She peered furtively about the room and lowered her voice. "I suspect a number of them left quite willingly. Some say there's a curse on Ashwood. After Garrett disappeared –"

"Who is Garrett?"

"One of the stable boys. Vanished from the face of the earth, he did. Not long before I came. Mary believes he fell into the hands of an evil spirit. But I *knew* Garrett" – presumably in the biblical sense. "I expect he ran away before he could be hauled on the carpet about the fire."

"And the others?"

"Who can say?" Alice shrugged. "I'm told Lady Margaret bent over backward to locate other positions for them." She frowned at the clock. "I should be getting along, miss. Whenever you wish a bath –"

"I wish one now. Now and every morning, please."

"Every morning? Yes, miss." She stalked out of the room, clearly horrified by my odd American habits.

The entry hall featured, among other items, a grandfather clock, and it struck eight as I entered the dining room. The same four places were set, but breakfast, I learned, was rather more casual than dinner: we served ourselves from the towering sideboard. Caitlin seemed unusually withdrawn; Mr. Carlisle distracted. Mrs. Ashworth, not surprisingly, pronounced her bacon, eggs, and porridge "tiresome."

I ate heartily, realizing that my opportunity

to do so represented a flaw in my hypothesis. The sideboard fairly groaned with food; if there was a financial crisis at Ashwood, surely the ham would be stricken from the breakfast menu. The kidneys. The kippers. And how strange about the servants. Why would *all* have resigned or been dismissed, then some replaced? Was it Mr. Carlisle's doing? Had he begun to "clean house" even before Edward's death?

"Did Mrs. Abbott show you round yesterday?" Mr. Carlisle interrupted my speculation.

"No, she didn't. I mean there was no chance," I amended quickly. If Mr. Carlisle was some sort of ogre, I didn't wish to suggest that Mrs. Abbott had been derelict in her duties. "We were quite exhausted when we arrived –"

"But you, at least, have staged a remarkable recovery." He eyed my ravished plate with a mischievous grin.

"Uh – yes."

"Are you up to a brief tour?"

"You're far too busy, Sean," Mrs. Ashworth cooed. "I shall guide Miss Hamilton –"

"Nonsense. I haven't a thing to do." Was there a bleak set to his mouth? "Miss Hamilton?"

"Miss Hamilton will no doubt want to spend the morning with – Mercy."

"Then *Mercy* will go with us."

Something had passed between them, something I could not fathom. At any rate, Mr. Carlisle dispatched a maid for Mercy, and a few minutes later the child skipped into the room – black hair shining, black eyes dancing – dangling Victoria by one porcelain arm. Foundering in a sea of propriety, I introduced "Aunt Caitlin," "Aunt Glynis," and "Mr. Carlisle."

"Cousin Sean," he corrected. "And may I propose that we dispense with all formality at once? It's bound to become exceedingly tiresome."

He sounded like Mrs. Ashworth, and I couldn't suppress a smile. His eyes met mine, and he smiled as well.

"I see no reason why we shouldn't use our Christian names; we are, in fact, related. If you're ready then, Linnet . . ."

We left the dining room, and I was acutely aware of Glynis's glittering green eyes on our backs.

We went first to the library, where Sean pointed out a priceless collection of first editions. Then:

"I really am curious about your life in the United States. I suppose I daren't hope you were attacked by Indians."

"Mercy asked the same thing."

"And?"

"Alas, no. As I explained to Mercy, I was a victim of civilization."

"You lived in New York then?"

"Chicago."

"Your father owned property there?"

"My father was a coachman." If Robin had kept it secret, Robin wasn't here to chastise me.

There was little of interest in the drawing room; the furnishings, though expensive, were uniformly modern. Sean did display a dagger which lay upon the mantel. According to legend, he said, it was a Saracen weapon brought home from the Crusades by an intrepid Ashworth ancestor.

"You're not an Ashworth," I said.

"No."

"Yet you're master of Ashwood. Are you qualified to administer an estate?" I bit my tongue, but it was too late; my ill-mannered question was bouncing off the velvet chairs, rippling through the damask drapes.

"My father had an estate in Norfolk."

"Oh? So did mine." If he wondered how a Norfolk squire had chanced to become a coachman in Chicago, Illinois, he was too

89

tactful to ask. "You were not the eldest son, I presume."

"The *only* son. But I sold the estate. Kilkenny, we called it. My mother was Irish."

"Mine half."

"Well, I expect we *are* cousins then. The Irish have very large families. There's a bedroom wing just there." He gestured to a corridor, which issued off the drawing room. "Glynis's and my quarters –"

Adjoin? As we drifted toward the music room, I conjectured why Sean Carlisle had disposed of his estate. Was he, like Father, a frustrated suitor of Lady Luck?

The music room contained, in addition to the ubiquitous piano, a harp, and Sean idly plucked the strings.

"Do you play?" he asked.

"I play nothing." The Coachman's Daughter was singularly unaccomplished.

"Mrs. Abbott plays," he said. "Isn't that astonishing? She has a very keen ear."

"Did you bring Mrs. Abbott from Norfolk?" It would account for the odd rearrangement of servants.

"No."

"Nor any of your other servants?"

"No. I sold Kilkenny several years ago, and the staff dispersed." He twanged the harp strings again. "Why do you ask?"

"I understood the servants at Ashwood were new."

"Umm," he grunted noncommittally. "Well, on to the picture gallery?"

The picture gallery was situated at the back of the house and extended the length of the main wing. Its ceiling was glass, and in brilliant natural light the Ashworths paraded through space and time – up one wall, down another, across a span of nearly four hundred years. Sean enlivened several of the portraits with personality sketches. Here was Henry – his hat magnificently plumed – who had served the eighth king of that name. Henry, like his sovereign, had been "extremely fond of the ladies." There were two dramatically divergent paintings of William. Appropriate, Sean remarked; William had frantically shifted his allegiance from king to Commonwealth and back, thereby preserving Ashwood throughout the Civil War. Elizabeth, splendidly bewigged, had been the first mistress of the present manor house. Elizabeth had been – "shall we say, generous with her favors?" and there was considerable doubt as to the legitimacy of the succeeding generation of Ashworths. Lady Margaret was forever frozen in early middle age; she resembled, except for her great black eyes, the miniature of my mother.

"And this is Edward."

He had borne a casual likeness to Sean; the hair and eyes were black, the skin dark. But the flattering portrait could not disguise the weakness of the chin, the uncertainty of the smile. "Tractable," Caitlin had said; I thought I would have guessed it.

Caitlin, realistically homely, appeared next, but there was a symmetrical space between her and Edward, and I glanced questioningly at Sean.

"Justin."

"And why was his picture removed?"

He shrugged. "Too painful for Aunt Margaret, I imagine."

Painful? Why should Justin's death be unbearably painful, Edward's not? I recalled Mrs. McDonald's hint of a family feud. It would explain Lady Margaret's relief that I had not known Justin, would explain Robin's – and my – "short shrift." Justin's conspicuous absence from the family shrine presented a whole new realm of possibilities, none of them particularly comforting. Sean was walking briskly toward a door at the back of the gallery, and I caught up with him just as he reached it.

"The gardens," he said.

His careless wave was an enormous understatement. I sucked in my breath and thought fleetingly of Ben Tyler, for the gardens of Ashwood truly reduced Mr. Parker's to nothing.

Did I say gardens? It was a miniature forest: acres of beech woods, with gravel pathways winding among the trees. I glimpsed statues here and there gleaming in the bright May sunlight and, far to the left, a waterfall and grotto. The trees ended – naturally it seemed – on the shore of a lake, and from the shore a narrow wooden bridge gave access to an island, which housed a tiny, perfect Greek temple. I did not want to venture closer, not ever, did not want to see the cracks in the shining walls, the flaws in the slender pillars.

Mercy – who had been scampering about us throughout our pilgrimage, alternately whining with boredom and shouting with glee – had no such compunctions. She raced through the woods and toward the bridge, Victoria bobbing precariously at her side.

"Mercy!"

"It's quite safe," Sean said. "I went over there once myself. I shan't go again. It's better from a distance."

I felt an eerie prickle at the base of my scalp, not because he had read my thoughts but because it seemed inevitable that he should. I watched as Mercy circled the pillars, disappearing, reappearing, rather like a May

93

Queen. She could be our child, I reflected. She had Sean's black hair and eyes, my fair complexion. Would all our offspring look like that? Or might there be one with dark skin and huge violet eyes?

Not that Sean Carlisle would wed a Coachman's Daughter. (*You are a Gentlewoman.* No, Father, I am nothing; neither fish nor fowl...) What difference did it make? Why did I stand there dreaming of marriage to a man I scarcely knew?

"Well," Sean said, "have you had enough? Shall we save the grand tour for another day?"

"The grand tour?"

"Yes. I shall take you round the tenant farms, and perhaps you'll learn to milk a cow. An art utterly beyond my fumbling fingers."

"Did Robin have the grand tour?"

"She requested as much. However, Mrs. Ashworth's excursion ended quite abruptly in the middle."

"Why was that?"

"She wasn't feeling well. A sudden illness, evidently; she looked in the peak of health when we went out."

"On horseback?" Robin had always detested horses.

"No, we took the gig."

"And at what point did Robin's – illness occur?"

"Umm." He frowned. "We visited Lakeview first. Mr. Stowe, the tenant there, has a splendid apiary, and Mrs. Ashworth seemed fascinated with the bees. We stopped briefly at Beech Meadow, but the tenant was away, so we went on to Long Hill Farm. And, yes, it was after we left Long Hill Farm that Mrs. Ashworth asked to return to the manor house. I suggested we take the indirect route so as to pass by the old mill, but Mrs. Ashworth said she wasn't up to it. She did appear most unwell."

His expression was altogether too innocent, and I couldn't determine whether he was conjuring up a host of unmentionable female maladies or whether he knew, with perfect certainty, the nature of Robin's "illness."

"Will you take me to Long Hill Farm?" I said impulsively.

"I'd rather not. Colin Hines was extremely annoyed at our intrusion. He's a touchy fellow, and I don't wish to poke my nose in where it isn't wanted. I'd be delighted to take you to Lakeview though . . ."

I wondered if Colin Hines had witnessed the event that had rendered Robin "dreadfully upset" and "most unwell."

"Not today, thank you," I said politely. "I believe I *have* had enough. If I can entice Mercy from her pagan temple –"

"Don't worry about her. I have to speak with the head gardener" – Sean nodded toward a grizzled man crouched in a budding bed of flowers – "and I'll keep an eye on her. She'll tire of her discovery soon enough."

I walked back through the house and up the stairs, my heart racing out of all proportion to the climb. What of my discovery? Was this Love – this flutter in the rib cage, this exhilaration, this sense of destiny untangling? If so, where would it lead me? Sean Carlisle was Lord of the Manor, I a Coachman's Daughter, and Glynis Ashworth stood between us . . .

The door of my room was ajar, and I scowled. I had nothing to hide, but Alice must be more careful. I stepped inside, glanced around, glowered at the bed. My portmanteau, which I had left under the bed, now rested on the counterpane. I lifted it and found it unaccountably heavy, then replaced it on the bed and opened it. All my possessions were within – everything but the clothes I wore – neatly packed, nothing missing.

Why? I stared at the black dress and the blue, the corsets and drawers and petticoats. Lady Margaret, for reasons I had yet to ascertain, was determined to be rid of us; that much was clear. But why had she employed such devious, if unsubtle, tactics? First she

96

had dispatched Caitlin with a vague warning of danger. Now she had directed someone (Caitlin again? Mary? Alice?) literally to pack my bags. Why did she not simply order us out of her home? Was she bound by some ancient code of hospitality? Or had Sean Carlisle, new master of Ashwood, forbidden any overtly hostile behavior? Had Sean even been consulted? He seemed amicable enough . . .

I idly caressed the silken folds of the black dress and pondered the advantages of a dignified retreat . . . and realized I had nowhere – nowhere else in all the world – to go.

FIVE

At dinner that evening Caitlin shyly invited me to join the family for church services the next morning. I had attended church but rarely in America; neither Mr. Parker nor Father had been particularly devout. I was framing a polite refusal when I observed Glynis glaring at Caitlin and decided perversely to accept.

We piled into the landau shortly after ten.

Glynis managed to wriggle in beside Sean, and Caitlin and I sat across from them. Sean took Mercy on his lap, which, to my delight, seemed to infuriate Glynis. Alf was in livery for the occasion, as was the groom on the box beside him, and we trotted out smartly, followed by two cartloads of servants.

I had pondered Lady Margaret's behavior until well after midnight but had drifted to sleep still torn between the Poverty Theory and the Feud Theory. The landau, I thought as we sped along the dusty road to Leatherhead, tended to favor the latter. We had been fetched from the station in a brougham, and Sean had mentioned a gig. There were two carts behind us. Five traps then and four draft horses: an elaborate equipage for a household teetering on the brink of bankruptcy.

The church was not unduly crowded, and, at any rate, we occupied the Ashworths' private pew. The sanctuary was hot, stuffy, and midway through the sermon Mercy fell asleep. Sean and I exchanged glances over her bowed black head, both wishing, I believe, that we might so readily escape our discomfort.

I fairly fled up the aisle after the benediction, but a milling, chattering throng had preceded me to the churchyard. I gazed in fascination at farm hands in smocks and top hats, country wives in starched dresses and matching sunbonnets, servants in holiday finery, neighboring squires and their elegant ladies. Did God see the scene as I did? I wondered. Did He see it at all? And, if so, where did He place me? Where did I belong?

Hines, looking suitably righteous in his customary black, was at the fringe of the crowd, deep in conversation with a young man. A "splendid-looking" young man of medium height, with brown hair gleaming gold in the sunlight. His son, no doubt. I felt a sudden ache in my rib cage, a sudden yearning for Father, and I walked quickly to the carriage.

After lunch I wrote a letter to Aunt Jane. I reported that I was "well" and compounded the lie by describing our "warm welcome" at Ashwood. I reserved my message for the third paragraph.

"You will be relieved to learn that Robin traveled from London to Ashwood. She was here for two days, then departed. I believe she might have gone on to visit relatives. As I have lost contact with our various cousins, etc., I should appreciate your sending a list of names . . ."

I penned a final sentence or two and signed myself "Your Loving Niece, Linnet."

I gave the letter to Alice after she had drawn my bath on Monday, and she assured me it would go out in the morning post.

"Was it Colin Hines I saw at St. Andrew's yesterday?" I asked as she turned to leave.

"The one talking to Mr. Hines? Yes, that was him all right. I'd just bid him good morning myself when Mr. Hines barged up and dragged him off." Alice's green eyes narrowed with annoyance. "Not that Colin Hines would look twice at a housemaid, but I was in hopes of meeting his hired hand."

"Was he there?" I had developed a voyeuristic interest in Alice's romantic entanglements – past, present, and projected.

"No." A moue of vexation. "Indeed I've never met the man. Rodman Thatcher. But Betsy says he's quite the handsomest fellow in the county."

"Betsy?"

"The maid at Long Hill Farm. There's no justice, Miss Hamilton." Alice set her arms akimbo. "Betsy's old enough to be my mother, widowed three times and ugly as sin if you'll pardon my saying so. And she's living at Long Hill Farm with two lovely bachelors while I –" She sighed.

I stifled a smile. "Where is Long Hill Farm?" I said casually.

"Two or three miles up the road."

"In which direction?"

"Away from Leatherhead. Are you thinking of visiting, miss?" Had Alice been a horse, she would have pawed the ground with enthusiasm.

"No, I was just curious."

"Oh." She visibly wilted. "Well, if you should change your mind, I'd be happy to go along. Just to keep you company of course."

"Of course."

Alice left, and I climbed into the hip bath, which had grown quite tepid.

By Tuesday I was writhing in an agony of boredom. Lady Margaret had apparently countermanded Mrs. Abbott's instructions, for Mary, not Alice, spent every waking hour with Mercy. On Sunday I found them – Mary, Mercy, and Victoria – "taking tea" in Mercy's room. It rained on Monday, and Mary filled Mercy's day with stories – ghost stories, I inferred from the scraps I overheard. When I stepped into the garden late Tuesday morning, I spotted Mary and Mercy on the steps of the island temple, a great picnic hamper between them.

How very odd, I mused, returning to the picture gallery. Had Lady Margaret undergone a change of heart? Surely she knew I had no experience of children; why had she chosen to spare me the potentially intolerable burden of Mercy's care? And why had she appointed her personal maid the instrument of my salvation?

Salvation? Perhaps Lady Margaret had shrewdly unsheathed her deadliest weapon: tedium. I glanced despairingly into the library. I had sniffed around its shelves and discovered them abounding in dusty tomes on a variety of scholarly topics – forbidding fruit for a casual reader of light novels. Sean was generally busy about the estate; Caitlin skulked in her room, scurrying out only at mealtimes; and Glynis had made no secret of her animosity. I had no one to talk to and – by Lady Margaret's grace – nothing to do. I could not continue aimlessly to wander through this Georgian mansion, and I wondered if Lady Margaret had sensed that and initiated a clever waiting game.

I decided impulsively to go to Long Hill Farm. "Touchy" Colin Hines would not welcome my trespass, but I doubted he'd toss me bodily off the property. And I might garner a clue as to what had transpired during Robin's visit.

Man-crazed Alice wasn't likely to aid my cause, so I crept through the main wing, searching for Hines. I came upon Mrs. Abbott in the dining room, where she was laying the sideboard for lunch.

"It isn't ready yet, Miss Hamilton," she said apologetically.

"I don't believe I shall have any lunch today. In fact, I was thinking" – I instinctively dissembled – "of taking a drive. I was looking for Hines –"

"Mr. Hines is in London."

"London?"

"Yes. He went up yesterday on a personal errand for Lady Margaret. But you can ask Alf to hitch a rig for you. Not that I approve of your missing lunch . . ."

Her lecture trailed me down the entry hall and through the front door. I was "exceedingly thin, unhealthily pale," she cautioned. "If you don't eat, I fear you'll waste away to nothing . . ." I left the house and followed the drive to the stable.

It was obviously new, and a blackened rectangle beside it indicated the scene of the lethal fire. I went inside and called for Alf but got no answer; evidently he and the grooms were at lunch. There were ten stalls. One was empty – Sean's saddle horse? I led out the bony bay who had met us at the station.

The coach house was deserted as well, and as I harnessed the mare to the gig, I noticed a gaily painted wagonette. Six traps, I amended, ten horses. Elaborate indeed.

The rain had freed the road of dust, but

I encountered few mud-spots, and I felt my spirits lifting as we clipped along. She was not one of Mr. Parker's trotters, of course, this gaunt mare . . . Mr. Parker. What would have happened to me if Father had lived? Would I have become a governess? Married an Impoverished Gentleman, a coachman perhaps? I would not have met Sean Carlisle . . .

No signpost marked the boundary of Long Hill Farm, and I slowed down after some fifteen minutes of driving. I soon glimpsed a man on horseback and pulled the mare to a halt.

"Hello!" I shouted. "Hello?"

He couldn't hear me, and I clambered out of the gig and tied the mare to a tree. I made my way across the field of ripening wheat, calling out from time to time, but a stiff breeze wafted my cries over my shoulder. It wasn't Colin Hines, I realized, drawing closer; the hair was too dark . . .

"Hello?"

He whirled in the saddle, his eyes wide with shock. "I'm sorry to have startled you." I had stopped perhaps three yards behind him. "I'm Miss Hamilton. Linnet Hamilton. I'm visiting at Ashwood . . ."

He stared at me for another moment, then dismounted and stepped forward. "Rodman

104

Thatcher," he said.

"Yes." Rodman? Mr. Thatcher? "Yes," I repeated lamely.

He was tall, thin, very dark, probably about Sean's age. I couldn't judge his alleged handsomeness because his face was lost in a thicket of hair – a black jungle of beard, mustache, and side-whiskers. But I thought, as I had with Caitlin, that he reminded me of someone.

"Miss Hamilton," I said again. "I was just driving around –"

"You have an accent. Canadian?"

"American, I suppose." Father would have been horrified. "I lived in the United States for many years."

"The United States? Were you –"

"I was never attacked by Indians."

"Umm."

We had tapped the dregs of our limited commonality.

"Well, the wheat looks good," I said brightly. "I mean, *does* the wheat look good?"

"I wish I could say, Miss Hamilton. I'm a novice farmer myself."

And what had he been before? I studied him surreptitiously. His clothes, though worn, were of excellent quality, his bearing confident, his accent cultured. The wind shifted, and I detected a sharp, sour odor.

Alcohol? An aristocrat who had drunk himself to hard times? His eyes met mine, and I flushed.

"I – uh – I wonder if you might perhaps have met my sister," I said.

"Today?" He seemed flustered.

"No. No, almost two weeks ago. She was with Mr. Carlisle."

"Mr. Carlisle." He wrinkled his forehead.

He was too circumspect by half. Was there a conspiracy afoot? Were they all in it together – Sean and Colin Hines and Rodman Thatcher?

"Yes," I snapped, "Mr. Carlisle. The squire, if I may refresh your memory. He recently brought my sister here – Mrs. Justin Ashworth. I know that for a fact. Now did you meet her?"

"No, I did not."

"But you saw her," I pressed.

"Now that you mention it, I believe I did. A woman of your coloring, but much smaller?"

Much smaller. I cursed my five feet seven inches and assumed what I hoped was a graceful slouch. "Yes, that was Robin. You didn't talk with her?"

"No."

"She had a lengthy conversation with Mr. Carlisle though," I suggested. "With Mr. Hines."

"I wouldn't know, Miss Hamilton. I was in the barn at the time and scarcely caught sight of them."

"And you heard nothing?" Heard no voices raised in anger?

"No, I –"

"Thatcher!"

The wind had muffled Colin Hines's approach; he loomed just over my shoulder, his gray horse dark with perspiration. He leaped out of the saddle and strode forward.

"Thatcher! What in the name of God do you think you're doing?" He nodded me a perfunctory apology. "You're not paid to gossip with every passing stranger."

Rodman Thatcher's black eyes flashed rebelliously. "I understand that, *Mr. Hines.*"

"Then if you have nothing better to do, perhaps you might see to Buttercup. She'll be calving any minute. If she hasn't already."

"Yes, *sir*. Good afternoon, Miss Hamilton."

Rodman Thatcher mounted his horse – rather awkwardly, I observed – and galloped furiously off. I transferred my attention to Colin Hines.

"We haven't been introduced," I said coldly. "I am Linnet Hamilton, Mrs. Justin Ashworth's sister."

"Yes," he mumbled absently. He mopped his brow with a limp, soiled handkerchief.

"I'm sorry to have distracted your hired hand. Mr. Thatcher was in no way responsible for our 'gossip.' I tied up my horse" – I gestured toward the mare standing patiently in the traces of the gig – "and ambushed him. Mr. Thatcher was merely trying to be polite –"

"Yes, yes." He waved his hand dismissingly, but I thought he had relented; he returned the handkerchief to his pocket.

"An unusual man, Mr. Thatcher," I said. "Has he worked for you long?"

"No, not long."

"What did he do before he came to Long Hill Farm?"

"I've no idea, Miss Hamilton. Farm hands come and go these days."

"I suppose so." I hesitated. "I believe my sister was here recently."

"That's right." His tone was casual, but he plucked the handkerchief once more from his pocket, and it fluttered, like a flag of truce, in the breeze.

"You spoke with her at some length, did you not?"

"Not really. I told her a bit about the farm and showed her the dairy, and then Mr. Carlisle and I got off on another matter, and she strolled about –"

"And nothing – unpleasant – occurred?"

"Unpleasant? Indeed not. If I may say so, your sister is a charming woman."

He had misconstrued my question. Deliberately?

"Did she seem ill when she left?" I asked.

"Umm. A trifle pale perhaps. It was a very warm day, as I recall." He swabbed his brow again. "Would *you* care to see the dairy, Miss Hamilton?"

He was fearfully anxious to be done with the subject of Robin. I debated his invitation for a moment, wondering whether Betsy would be at the dairy. If so, would she be of any help? Doubtful; if she knew anything of Robin's visit, she had surely been intimidated to silence.

"Thank you, no," I said. "Perhaps some other time —"

"Of course, of course." His relief was manifest. "I'll walk along to your trap then."

"That won't be necessary. Good day, Mr. Hines."

I drove back to Ashwood at a leisurely pace, convinced that there had been a quarrel at Long Hill Farm. Colin Hines had witnessed it, and I suspected Rodman Thatcher had as well. The situation struck me as exceedingly strange. Robin had always been the soul of propriety, and Sean Carlisle seemed discreet enough. Why would they air their differences

109

in front of a tenant farmer and a hired hand?

Alf was dozing outside the stable when I arrived, and several minutes elapsed before he became sufficiently alert to relieve me of the gig and the mare. The grandfather clock was chiming three as I stepped into the entry hall; an hour yet till tea, and my stomach was rumbling with hunger. I walked toward the kitchen, hoping to beg a "treat" from Mrs. Abbott.

The kitchen lay just off the dining room, and the doors were open. Hines had obviously returned from London, for he and Mrs. Abbott were engaged in one of their perennial altercations. Rose (a laundry maid) must mend her ways, Hines was saying sternly.

"Miss Hamilton!" Mrs. Abbott bounded out of her chair, clearly welcoming the interruption. "You had a pleasant drive, I trust?"

"Yes, but –"

"You're hungry. And small wonder. One should never skip lunch, Miss Hamilton." She wagged a plump, admonitory finger. "Fortunately, the tea things are all ready. Some nice cucumber sandwiches, some scones, some little cakes . . ."

As she bustled about, I idly noted the enormous range, the dresser, the copper and iron cookware adorning the walls. Hines was seated at an ancient oak table, primly sipping a cup of tea.

"Well, now, will this tide you over?" Mrs. Abbott displayed a plate positively heaped with food. "And would you be wanting tea or lemonade?"

"Lemonade, please."

I sat at the table, and Mrs. Abbott raised her eyebrows, recovered herself, set the plate before me. A faux pas, I realized wearily, wolfing down a cucumber sandwich. I was a guest at Ashwood, and guests did not mingle with the servants. I have betrayed you again, Father . . .

"There." Mrs. Abbott deposited a glass of lemonade next to the plate and resumed her own chair. "A pleasant drive, you say? And where did you go?"

I paused between bites and looked up. "To Long Hill Farm."

Hines was sitting directly across from me, and he started, his cup frozen midway between saucer and mouth.

"Long Hill Farm?" Mrs. Abbott, unaware of Hines's reaction, went cheerfully on. "Did you run across Mr. Hines's son then?"

"Briefly. He happened along as I was talking to Rodman Thatcher –"

Hines dropped his cup. It hit the matching saucer, splitting the latter neatly in half, then rolled on its side, trickling the last few drops of tea onto the table. "Now see what you've done!" Mrs. Abbott jumped to her feet. "Say what you will about Rose – at least the girl isn't clumsy."

She stalked across the room, muttering imprecations under her breath, and came back with a towel. Hines stood up.

"Please excuse me, Miss Hamilton," he said stiffly. "I must – must –" His explanation trailed off, and he hurried out of the kitchen.

Mrs. Abbott completed her mopping-up and sat down again. "Isn't that just like a man? Mr. Hines would fairly have a stroke if one of the maids was to smash up the crockery and dribble tea about –"

"He seemed upset," I interrupted. Was Hines yet another conspirator?

"Did he? Well, Mr. Hines is very sensitive about his son."

"Colin?"

"Yes."

"And why is that?"

"I really shouldn't say." Mrs. Abbott briskly stirred her tea.

"Why on earth not?"

She peered nervously toward the doors, now closed. "I got it from my sister," she hissed.

"Your sister?"

"She was a kitchen maid at Ashwood some twenty years ago," she whispered.

"So?"

"Please don't mention it, Miss Hamilton. If Lady Margaret knew, she'd toss me out in an instant."

"Why?"

"It was a condition of the recent hiring. Lady Margaret wanted no one at Ashwood who'd been here before. Nor anyone with relatives previously employed. The word got round, of course, and when I interviewed, I fibbed a bit. It's been twenty years, after all, and Maude was at Ashwood a month or two at most. Then she married a railroad man and went to live in London. You won't say anything, will you, Miss Hamilton?"

"No, I won't say anything." I demolished the final cake. "What did Maude tell you about Colin Hines?"

"That Sir Robert singled him out for special treatment." Apparently confident of our privacy, Mrs. Abbott spoke in normal tones. "Colin was twelve or thirteen at the time. Mrs. Hines was long since dead, and Colin – says Maude – was terribly wild. Had nothing whatever to recommend him. But Sir Robert – out of the blue – decided to send him to public school. A shot in the dark, as they say, but it found its mark; Colin proved

113

an exceptional student."

"But Hines is embarrassed by Sir Robert's generosity. Sees it as charity, I suppose."

"There's more, Miss Hamilton. After Colin left school, he went up to London and secured a post in a brewery. A clerical position, I believe, but he moved right up, and eventually he was all but running the place. And then, very suddenly, Lady Margaret ejected the tenant from Long Hill Farm and brought Colin down in his stead."

"When was this?"

"Umm. Two months since? About the time I came to Ashwood."

"What happened to the prior tenant?"

"I understand Lady Margaret got him a place in Sussex."

So it was Lady Margaret who had engineered the restaffing of Ashwood. Not out of necessity, it seemed. Out of grief? Had she wished to sever all ties, however remote, with the past? Then why had Hines and Alf been retained? And why had Colin, "all but running" a brewery, agreed to return to the country?

"So Colin Hines knows nothing about farming," I said aloud.

"He has no *experience*." Mrs. Abbott drained her teacup. "But he's fearfully bright, and I'm sure Mr. Carlisle is keeping a sharp eye on him. You needn't worry on that account, Miss Hamilton."

"On what account?" I asked absently, downing a wayward crumb.

"That the estate will fall to pieces during the regency, so to speak. Everything will be in good order when Miss Mercy reaches her majority. God willing, she'll have a husband by then . . ."

Regency? Majority? "What are you trying to say, Mrs. Abbott?"

"Why, just that Mr. Carlisle will look after Miss Mercy's interests."

"And what interests are those?"

"Well, you'd know that better than I, now wouldn't you? I don't understand bonds and shares and that sort of thing. It seems enough to me that Miss Mercy is mistress of Ashwood."

SIX

I sensed I would learn nothing more if I revealed my shock, and I managed a serene smile.

"Yes, I have implicit confidence in Mr. Carlisle," I said. "He seems most conscientious. Though I must confess –" I allowed my voice to taper off.

"Confess what?" Mrs. Abbott pressed eagerly.

"That I have never understood the precise details of the bequest. Mercy's great-aunt was necessarily vague –"

"Well, that's easy enough. The estate would have gone to Mr. Ashworth's heir if he'd had one. But he specified that if he died childless, Ashwood was to revert to Dr. Ashworth or *his* heir. And, in either case, if the heir was a minor child, Mr. Ashworth appointed his cousin Mr. Carlisle to administer the estate till the child reached legal age."

"I see. Mr. Ashworth composed this will shortly before he died, I assume."

"Oh, no, miss. No, he wrote it just after he himself inherited Ashwood. Just after Sir Robert died. Which would have been –"

"Ten years ago. Long after your sister left Ashwood, Mrs. Abbott."

"Oh, yes, long after that."

"Then how did you come to know the contents of the will?"

She flushed brick red. "I – I – well – there was some discussion –" She gulped furiously from her empty teacup.

"Which you overheard."

"I don't make a habit of eavesdropping,

Miss Hamilton," she said defensively. "But I'm not deaf, am I, and there was a good bit of shouting –"

"What was the gist of the shouting?"

"I'd rather not say. It's all in the past."

I summoned my coldest stare, and she relented.

"Oh, all right. Lady Margaret and Mrs. Ashworth wanted Mr. Ashworth to change his will. It was a terrible thing, it was – the poor man literally on his deathbed, and them badgering him day in and day out."

"In what way did they want the will changed?"

"Well, Mrs. Ashworth would have loved to get her pretty hands on the estate, of course, but that was out of the question. So what they proposed – she and Lady Margaret – was that Ashwood go directly to Mr. Carlisle. He *is* Mr. Ashworth's closest male relative, as they were fond of pointing out. I believe Mr. Ashworth eventually agreed, for Lady Margaret summoned a solicitor down from London. But by the time he arrived, Mr. Ashworth had lapsed into a coma, and he died without regaining consciousness."

My Irish temper was approaching a boil. How dare she? I marveled furiously. Thwarted in her efforts to revise Edward's will, Lady Margaret had elected simply to

117

ignore it, had attempted to cast Mercy out of her own home ... I rose, snarled an excuse, and left Mrs. Abbott still lamenting the trials of "poor Mr. Ashworth." I stalked down the corridor to Lady Margaret's room.

"Come in, Mary." Lady Margaret answered my knock in her deep, melodious voice.

"It isn't Mary, ma'am." I closed the door behind me and leaned against it.

Lady Margaret – in a gray dressing gown this time – was sitting up in her curtained bed, pen in hand, notepaper scattered on the sickroom tray in front of her. Her ravaged face flickered surprise, and then she flashed her terrible smile.

"Miss Hamilton. How very fortunate. I had thought to send for you after dinner, but I can well understand your impatience."

It was not the greeting I had expected, and I ventured only a tentative step away from the door. "Impatience?" I echoed uncertainly.

"This isn't the place for a young woman, is it? I worry so about Caitlin. How the child is ever to meet a suitable prospect, secluded in the country as she is. ..." Lady Margaret sighed. "Nor would Mercy fare any better. No, much as I love Ashwood, I sympathize with your desire to establish a city household. To that end –"

She was infinitely cleverer than I, I

118

conceded. She had shoved words into my mouth, thoughts into my head, and had nearly convinced me that they were mine.

"The only city household we talked about was Robin's, Lady Margaret."

"Oh? Then I must have inferred your feelings. There was a question of money, as I recall." She cleared her throat delicately.

"Yes, there was a question of money. However, certain facts have come to my attention –"

"What facts?" Lady Margaret said sharply.

"*Fact*, I should have said. That Mercy inherited Ashwood."

My response triggered some deep emotion; I saw her face twitch. But when she spoke, her tone was noncommittal. "So she did."

"Then she has every right to be here. And to stay. I shall locate a maid for her, a governess –"

"You will do nothing of the kind, Miss Hamilton." There were bright slashes of color high on her cheeks. "I thought I had made myself perfectly clear on that account. Mercy *cannot* remain at Ashwood. I am therefore prepared to offer a generous settlement –"

"Did you offer Robin a settlement as well?"

"Your sister and I did not discuss the matter. As I indicated before, her visit was strictly one of courtesy."

119

Her great black eyes defied me to disbelieve her, and I lowered my own. "What sort of settlement did you have in mind?" I asked.

"Twenty thousand pounds." The words rolled sonorously off her tongue, lest the magnitude of her largesse escape me. "I'm sure I needn't tell you it's a great deal of money. Sufficient for the two of you to live quite comfortably for many years."

"The two of us? And what of Robin?"

Lady Margaret hesitated. "Has it not occurred to you, Miss Hamilton, that your sister has no intention of resuming her maternal responsibilities?"

"That she has abandoned Mercy, you mean?"

"Yes." Her voice was heavy with regret.

"I have considered the possibility," I admitted. "But any such conclusion would be exceedingly premature. She departed Ashwood less than two weeks since –"

"I shan't argue the point." Lady Margaret waved one slender, white hand. "If Robin returns, the settlement will be adjusted accordingly. An additional ten thousand pounds, shall we say?"

Twenty thousand pounds. Perhaps thirty. As Lady Margaret had said, a great deal of money. Yet probably but a small fraction of Mercy's ultimate prospects.

"I shall have to think it over," I said carefully.

"There is nothing to think over, Miss Hamilton." An unpleasant note had crept beneath Lady Margaret's cultivated tones. "You have no alternative —"

"I beg your pardon, Lady Margaret." My temper flared again. "It is you who have no alternative. Mercy is mistress of Ashwood, and I am her guardian."

"Are you now, Miss Hamilton?" Her half-smile was cruel around the edges. "You have legal documents to substantiate your position?" My silence answered her in the negative. "Then I suspect Caitlin's claim might well prove stronger than yours. Caitlin's or indeed my own. You are virtually a foreigner, with no means of support . . . No, I very much fear a court of law would rule against you."

Would it? I needed help, I realized, a bolt of reason penetrating my rage. Needed time. And Lady Margaret would give me time only if she believed she had won.

"You misunderstood me, Lady Margaret," I said smoothly. "I have no wish to place Mercy where she isn't wanted. But I shall require a few days to evaluate the figure. I *am*, after all, a foreigner." I attempted to emulate Mr. Parker's American drawl.

121

"Twenty thousand pounds *sounds* like a lot, but I'm not familiar with the cost of living in England. If I might work up a budget . . ."

"Oh, very well." Her waxen visage turned grouchy, but studiedly so; she had anticipated a hard bargain. "But I shall permit you forty-eight hours, no more. Draw up your budget and return to me on Thursday evening . . ."

There was an interlude of idle conversation; Lady Margaret, victorious, could afford a moment of courtesy. She dismissed me at last, and I rushed to my room, my frantic impressions assuming a semblance of order.

First, a letter to Giles Chapman, via Aunt Jane.

"I do not know Mr. Chapman's address," I scrawled on the covering note, "so please, *please* forward this communication without delay. It is imperative that he be acquainted with my circumstances at once."

I employed a rather more reserved tone with Mr. Chapman himself:

Mr. Leighton may have informed you that I have brought my niece to her paternal grandmother. The situation here is most confusing. Mercy, I have learned, inherited her uncle's estate, but her grandmother, Lady Margaret Ashworth, is pressing me to accept a cash settlement

122

in lieu of Ashwood. Lady Margaret has also suggested that I have no legal claim to Mercy's guardianship.

I am utterly at a loss, Mr. Chapman, and sorely require legal advice. Might you travel down from London and spend a day with me? If not, I should much appreciate a letter of guidance. In either event, I must stress that time is of the essence.

I cannot predict when you might be paid for your efforts; I remain, however,

Your grateful servant,
Miss Linnet Hamilton

I rammed the letter and accompanying note into an envelope and yanked the bell rope. Some ten minutes elapsed before Alice, red hair spilling untidily around her face, breathlessly answered my summons.

"Yes, miss? I was tied up in the stable, I was . . ."

Tied up? Not, I thought dryly, a literal description of her recent circumstances. "I have a letter to be posted, Alice." I thrust the envelope into her freckled hands. "I want it to go out as soon as possible."

"Well, you've missed the afternoon post, Miss Hamilton."

"I suppose it will have to wait till morning then."

"As a matter of fact, Alf is driving to town tomorrow. Very early, he said." She glanced at the address on the envelope. "Perhaps he could get it on the first train –"

"Alf?" I said doubtfully.

"He may not be bright, but he's quite dependable," Alice said stiffly. Was it Alf she'd been tumbling in the stable? "Though Mr. Hines dressed him down this afternoon, that's for certain."

"Dressed him down about what?" I asked absently.

"I can't rightly say. It was almost over when I got there, and poor Alf couldn't remember. But he'll see your letter on its way; I promise you that, miss."

I waved her off and pondered the next step. Lady Margaret had demanded an answer Thursday night, and I could not hope to hear from Giles Chapman before Friday. Time enough, I decided. During the course of my meeting with Lady Margaret I would announce that I had retained a solicitor, due at Ashwood on the morrow. She was unlikely to launch a new attack under the very nose of a powerful city lawyer. Powerful? I envisioned Giles Chapman in all his mouselike splendor and shuddered. Would he prove any match for Lady Margaret? Would he even consent to advise me? And, if not, where was I to turn?

It was just after six by the mantel clock –
almost an hour to dinner. I collapsed into
the Queen Anne armchair near the window
and reviewed my conversation with Lady
Margaret.

Robin, she insisted, had not come to
Ashwood to discuss Mercy's inheritance.
Which, if true, could only mean that Robin
did not know the terms of Edward's will. Was
that possible? Could Justin have neglected –
through eight years of marriage, through the
months of Edward's fatal illness – to mention
that he was his brother's heir? No. Then
Robin must have failed to draw the corollary:
that if Justin predeceased Edward, the estate
would go to Mercy. Otherwise she would have
returned immediately to London and engaged
a solicitor in Mercy's behalf.

So it appeared my earlier surmise was
correct: Robin had journeyed down to ask
for money – charity, she believed. She had
quarreled with Lady Margaret, quarreled
with Sean, been sent away. Why? Why was
Lady Margaret prepared to give me twenty
thousand pounds or more, Robin nothing?
Had she thought to keep Robin forever in
the dark about the bequest? Then why had
she allowed me to discover the truth? The
threat of discharge would have sealed even
Mrs. Abbott's loose lips.

Why, above all, was Lady Margaret so desperate to be rid of Mercy? While twenty thousand pounds might represent an insignificant portion of the Ashworths' assets, in cash it was an enormous sum. Could they not plunder the estate for that much and more over the fourteen years of Mercy's minority? Or was that just the point; did they fear my interference? And who were "they"? Was Sean a party to his aunt's machinations? Glynis?

As a consequence of my emotional turmoil (or maybe a surfeit of cucumber sandwiches) I was able only to pick at my dinner. When Glynis, seductively clad in clinging, apple-green silk, rose from the table, I excused myself and wandered into the garden.

It was a beautiful night: the moon was nearly full, and the air – warm but not close – smelled of growing things. I ambled along one of the gravel pathways, thinking of Ben Tyler. How simple life would have been if I'd married him! We would have a cozy room in Mr. Parker's house, a child on the way perhaps . . .

I stopped in front of a statue of Zeus. Did God look like him? I wondered. Or were they one? If I knelt and prayed to this stern, marble deity, would God hear me?

"Are you a pagan then, Linnet?"

Sean's voice startled me but not his words;

I had grown accustomed to the eerie bond between us. I turned and found him smiling at me in the moonlight.

"I really don't know what I am," I said.

He was silent for a moment. "Not a Greek goddess, I'm afraid. They were all quite strapping, weren't they?"

"I believe they were."

Was he in league with Lady Margaret? His face was inscrutable, dappled in silver light and dancing shadow.

"Actually, I was assessing the statue," I said impulsively.

"Assessing it?"

"Yes. Wondering what it's worth. What is Ashwood worth, Sean?"

"Are you thinking of selling it?" he parried.

"Is it mine to sell?"

"You'd have to prove me an unfit trustee. Which might not be difficult to do." His teeth flashed in a crooked grin.

"Suppose I did. Prove you unfit, that is. Should I take twenty thousand pounds for it?"

"For Ashwood? Good God, no. It'd fetch ten times that, I expect. Did someone offer you twenty thousand pounds?"

"In a manner of speaking."

"A local man?"

"A local woman. I'm referring to Lady

Margaret's settlement."

"What settlement is that?"

Was he dissembling? The moon had slipped behind a wayward cloud, and I couldn't tell.

"Lady Margaret has offered me twenty thousand pounds, in return for which I'm to remove Mercy from Ashwood and surrender any further claim to the estate. Should I accept?"

He hesitated again. "That depends, doesn't it? On what you were seeking when you came here –"

"I was seeking nothing," I interrupted angrily. "Nothing beyond a home for Mercy –"

"And yourself?"

"I shall manage very nicely," I said icily.

"Ah. You left a suitor pining away in America then."

"That is no concern of yours."

"But it is. If Mercy stays on, she'll need a governess, and I'd hoped to entice you into the post."

I almost laughed aloud at the irony of it. Had I traveled thousands of miles only to become a governess after all?

"My plans are indefinite at present," I said, remembering Giles Chapman. "I shall consider it . . ."

"Yes, write your young man."

"There is no young man!"

"Splendid."

He gave me a mocking bow and retreated up the path, and my eyes followed him into the picture gallery. He and Lady Margaret had not conspired: she wanted me gone from Ashwood; he wished me to remain. But I suspected that his motives – if different – were no less devious than hers.

SEVEN

In my eagerness to communicate with Mr. Chapman, I had forgotten my earlier letter to Aunt Jane. I was sprawled in my armchair, staring at the mantel clock and glumly counting off the minutes till tea, when Alice delivered the yield of the Wednesday afternoon post.

"A letter from London," she trilled. She looked quite presentable today; apparently she had managed to resist the lure of the stable. "The correspondence is fairly flying back and forth, isn't it, miss?" She winked broadly.

I hadn't the heart to dash her romantic fancies. "Did Alf put my letter on the

129

morning train?" I asked.

"Yes, miss, the first one. Poor Alf." She sighed. "When he got back, he was blessed out again, he was."

"Because of the letter?"

"Oh, no, miss. He forgot Lady Margaret's medicine."

"Is Lady Margaret ill?"

"Not seriously. Something's making the rounds – a stomach complaint, I'm told. The grooms were sick a week since . . ."

Alice described the symptoms in rather more detail than I might have wished, and eventually excused herself. I opened Aunt Jane's letter and found it quite brief:

I have no report of Robin. I sent Douglas to Spring Street yesterday morning, but Mrs. McDermott [sic] has not heard from her either. While I was relieved to learn of her visit to Ashwood, I cannot imagine where she has gone to from there. Uncle John, your father's namesake, died childless many years ago. Your mother, as you know, had no siblings. She occasionally referred to cousins in Ireland, but I do not believe she corresponded with them. Nor, so far as I am aware, did Robin.

So I think it highly unlikely that your sister is with relatives. I would advise you

130

to redirect your inquiries so as to locate a friend.

The final word fairly dripped with innuendo. I read a closing paragraph of polite banalities and tossed the letter aside.

Back to the lover then. Much as I longed to believe otherwise, I was forced to conclude that Aunt Jane and Lady Margaret were right; that Robin's fruitless trip to Ashwood had been the last of her parental endeavors; that she had – temporarily at least – abandoned Mercy. I penned a note to Mrs. McDonald, informing her, "Mrs. Ashworth no longer requires your services," and enclosed a five-pound note, suspecting it was far too much.

On Thursday I woke to the spatter of rain on my window. I pulled the damask drapes aside and beheld an exceedingly bleak scene: gray skies, fog, and a suggestion of chilliness. Alice brought my bath and with it news: Lady Margaret was much improved, but Mary had been struck down by the epidemic.

"She was throwing up all over the place, she was. And off to the water closet every five minutes –"

"I'm sorry to hear that, Alice," I interrupted, somewhat queasy myself. "I'm sure she'll be better by tomorrow."

"But that leaves today, doesn't it, miss?"

"Leaves today for what?" I gazed wistfully at the rapidly cooling bath.

"Well, Mrs. Abbott has asked me to look after Miss Mercy. And the fact is, I had plans." Alice's smoldering eyes and flushed cheeks left little doubt about what these plans consisted of.

"I'll take care of Mercy," I said. A constructive enterprise at last.

"I'd be eternally grateful, miss. And it might be best if Mrs. Abbott wasn't to know . . ."

Mercy greeted me with a notable lack of enthusiasm.

"Where's Mary?" she demanded.

"Mary is sick. But I'm sure we'll find all sorts of exciting things to do —"

"Mary was going to tell us a story," Mercy said petulantly. She patted Victoria's head and repositioned the doll on her lap.

"What kind of story?"

"A story about the ghost of Ashwood." Mercy shivered in anticipation.

"I didn't realize Ashwood had a ghost."

"Of course it does," Mercy sniffed. "A man who creeps through the gardens in the dead of night. Mary thinks it's the duke."

"What duke?"

"The duke who lived here years ago. Years and years and years —"

132

"Well, I know a wonderful story about a sleeping princess . . ."

Not nearly wonderful enough. Mercy was fidgeting even as the thorns encircled the princess's bedchamber and stood up long before the prince could plant his magic kiss. She proposed a game, a game in which I was to portray a wicked witch. It was the first of many roles. I was, in turn, the witch, an evil stepmother, the Queen of the Goblins, and, as I recall, a vicious she-bear. When Alice, disheveled and beaming, delivered Mercy's dinner, I staggered back to my room, mumbling a prayer for Mary's early recovery.

After dinner Sean declined Glynis's invitation to another musicale, and she flounced into the music room, shepherding Caitlin along in front of her. I lingered at the table, awaiting Lady Margaret's summons. Ten minutes passed, and I wondered if she had forgotten her ultimatum. Or, with Mary "throwing up all over the place," was she without a servant to fetch me? I paced the entry hall while the grandfather clock marked ten minutes more. Enough: I had steeled myself for this confrontation, and I didn't want it postponed. I strode resolutely down the narrow hall to Lady Margaret's quarters.

I had cocked my fist to knock when I detected a murmur of voices beyond the door. I glanced furtively over my shoulder, then laid an ear to one carved panel.

"Twenty thousand pounds is nothing," Lady Margaret hissed. "Nothing."

"But it must come from somewhere." Sean. I pressed closer to the door.

"I have made the necessary arrangements. It is not your concern."

"I'm afraid it is, Aunt Margaret. Need I remind you that Ashwood is my responsibility?"

"Indeed you need not. It makes your behavior all the more incomprehensible. She was willing to come to terms, and now you've spoiled everything. I shall have to back down. Governess!" She spat. "They must be got rid of; can't you see that? It's to your advantage as much as my own —"

"Perhaps I view my advantage differently."

There was a stir of movement, and I stepped away and strolled casually up the corridor. I would claim I had heard voices, nothing more. . . . But I reached the entry hall without incident and proceeded up the stairs to my room.

An intriguing conversation, I mused, donning my nightgown. It tended to confirm my guess that Lady Margaret hoped to pillage the estate. Recognized me as an impediment. Had "made the necessary arrangements" to remove me. A sensible scheme, yet Sean had demurred. Why? What was his advantage, his "different" advantage? How did Sean Carlisle stand to profit if he persuaded me to stay at Ashwood?

The ticking of the mantel clock lulled me to uneasy sleep.

Mrs. Abbott herself laid our breakfast on the sideboard, muttering. "All the maids are sick. All of them. A puny lot, I'm sorry to say . . ." I fortified myself with a double serving of eggs, half hoping Mercy might have succumbed to the rampant infection.

She had not. She was stationed in the entry hall in front of the grandfather clock, teaching Victoria to tell time. "When the big hand lies at twelve . . ." I sighed.

"We want to go someplace," Mercy whined, evidently despairing of Victoria's education.

"Go where?"

"To France."

"Well, we can't go to France today. However" – an inspiration – "I shall take you to Long Hill Farm."

"Is that where the duke lives?"

"Perhaps. We can look for him, can't we?"

"I believe the duke is hiding out at Lakeview," Sean said smoothly. He had crouched at Mercy's side and was bouncing Victoria on his knee. "I'm occupied today, but we shall all drive over tomorrow."

"Are we not to go to Long Hill Farm then?" I asked sharply.

Sean rose and returned Victoria to Mercy's outstretched arms. "I thought I mentioned that Colin Hines is a trifle touchy –"

"But Mercy has every right to visit the farm, doesn't she?" I said pointedly.

"I suppose she does."

"Then if you would see to a trap –"

Sean slammed out the front door, and Mrs. Abbott – who was hovering in the dining-room archway – sent Mercy upstairs for a bonnet.

"Which you need as well, miss," she admonished me sternly. "The sun does terrible things to one's skin. Thin as you are, you mustn't be red and freckled to boot . . ."

I let her chatter on, not choosing to confess that I owned only one hat – a demure black, purchased for the occasion of Father's funeral. Mercy reappeared sporting a bonnet half a size too small. Victoria had been outfitted with headgear as well – a floppy chapeau fashioned of yellowing newspapers.

Alf had successfully hitched the gig and was exercising the horse outside the coach house. (A black gelding this time, again no champion.) I told Alf we would return in some two hours and clucked the aging eunuch to a start.

The rain had ended during the night, but the road had yet to dry, and the gig lurched from side to side as I attempted to avoid a profusion of mud puddles. Mercy was entranced with the scenery and, of course, hastened to share her observations with Victoria. Still within sight of Ashwood, she identified a dilapidated cottage as "The ogre's house": "You remember the ogre, Victoria, the one who eats children?" Mercy shuddered. Further horrors awaited us: A gnarled tree that was actually a prince transformed by an evil spell; a pond in whose depths a merman lurked, enticing unsuspecting passersby to a watery grave. I valiantly ignored the initial twinges of a headache.

"Ohhh!"

Mercy squealed with delight as the gig careened around a puddle. I felt a pleasant jolt in the pit of my stomach and laughed along with her. Then I realized that the gig was not responding as it should: rather than righting itself, it was dipping ever closer to the road. I frantically tugged the reins, and the gelding stopped just as they slipped from my hands. I closed my eyes instinctively, and there was a sickening crash, a stab of pain in my right shoulder, a sticky dampness beneath my cheek. I opened my eyes and found myself half in the gig, half in the road, Mercy sprawled on top of me.

"Are you all right, Mercy?" I asked weakly.

"What happened?"

"I don't know, dear. But you must get out first. Carefully now; just climb up over the side."

Fortunately, she was very light, and I scarcely felt her tiny feet on my hip as she clambered out of the gig. I struggled upright and joined her in the road, where she was clutching a miraculously unscathed Victoria to her breast.

"Are you all right?" I repeated.

"Oh, yes. May we do it again, Aunt Linnet?"

"I think not."

I quickly assessed our situation. The right-hand wheel of the gig lay perhaps twenty feet from the overturned vehicle. The rig itself appeared undamaged, as did Mercy, Victoria, and the horse, who was placidly devouring a patch of grass at the side of the road. I swiped at my cheek and examined my fingers; the moisture I had feared to be blood was mud alone. I gingerly massaged my shoulder and diagnosed it only bruised. Father's faithless consort, Lady Luck, had smiled upon us.

"Well, we shall have to hike back to Ashwood," I said cheerfully.

"Walk? But Victoria is tired —"

"Then I shall take Victoria," I snapped.

I tied the gelding to a sagging fence rail, and we ventured back down the road, presenting, I expect, a most comical picture. Mercy led the way, missing not a single puddle, fairly wallowing in the muck which already encrusted her boots and skirt. Spattered with mud from forehead to toe, I trudged in her wake, shifting Victoria from hand to hand. When we reached the gatehouse, Mercy reclaimed Victoria and dashed up the drive, leaving me to pant along far behind her.

I encountered Alice just outside the stable.

"Why, you look a fright, miss," she gasped. She, I noted silently, was hardly a study in grooming. "I suppose you'll be wanting a bath right away —"

"Right away," I confirmed grimly. "Meanwhile —"

Meanwhile a handsome young groom had materialized at Alice's side, his arm possessively encircling her waist. A veritable saint, I thought irritably, to have restored

139

Alice so rapidly to health ... I briefly described the accident and the spot where I had left the gelding, then turned to go.

"I almost forgot, Miss Hamilton." Alice caught me up. "You have a guest."

"A guest? I?"

"Yes. A young man from London."

Her expression was one of keen disappointment, and my heart bounded. Giles Chapman, my unlikely knight in armor, had arrived.

A muted hum of voices issued from the drawing room, and I paused for a moment on the threshold. Mr. Chapman was seated on a velvet sofa, Caitlin beside him, and I saw at once who it was she had reminded me of. There was scarcely a foot between them, and even as I watched, Mr. Chapman laughed and further reduced the distance. Ah, Alice, perhaps you shall have a romance after all. I cleared my throat and strode into the room.

"Miss Hamilton!" Giles Chapman sprang guiltily to his feet, and I suppressed a chuckle. "I received your letter only yesterday, and I came as soon as I could –"

"I'm grateful, Mr. Chapman. You've met Miss Ashworth, I see?"

"Uh – yes." He blushed. "We've had quite a long chat, in fact. I must just have missed you. You went for a drive, I understand . . ." He straightened his spectacles, took in my disgraceful appearance, and lapsed into awkward silence.

"Please forgive me." I stroked my filthy skirt. "We had a minor accident –"

"Accident?" Caitlin interjected shrilly. "What sort of accident?"

"It was nothing really. The gig lost a wheel –"

"Oh, dear." Caitlin turned ashen, and her hands, primly folded in her lap, began to tremble. "Oh, dear."

"It was nothing, Caitlin," I insisted. "No one was injured, not even Mercy's doll –"

"I – you must excuse me." She rose and walked unsteadily across the room. "Perhaps you'll come again, Mr. Chapman. Yes, I do hope so –" She tripped over her skirt as she fled into the entry hall.

Oh, Caitlin. A "suitable prospect," and you've bungled it . . .

"I'm afraid she might be ill," I said conspiratorially. "We've had a bit of an epidemic here."

"Ill. Yes."

Mr. Chapman was frowning at the archway, and I hastened to distract him. "I do so appreciate your assistance. It was an inconvenience, I know –"

"No, Miss Hamilton, truly it wasn't. As it happens, I have a client in Leatherhead, and I enjoy a jaunt to the country at any rate."

"Shall I ring for tea?"

"Tea?" He dragged his eyes from the archway. "No, no, thank you."

"Well, let's sit down then, and I shall fill you in."

I took Caitlin's place on the sofa, and Mr. Chapman, I was pleased to observe, perched discreetly on the opposite end. I reviewed the particulars of Edward's will and related what I knew of Robin's visit to Ashwood. "She quarreled with each of them in turn – Mr. Carlisle and Lady Margaret. I can only assume these disagreements concerned money. Robin left –"

"And you don't know where she is?"

"No, I do not. I wrote Aunt Jane – Mrs. Leighton – but she's quite as puzzled as I."

"Go on then."

I detailed Lady Margaret's initial hostility, her subsequent proposal and accompanying threats. "So," I concluded, "as I indicated in my letter, I am at a loss. I want to do what's best for Mercy."

"You've told me everything?" he said.

His voice seemed firmer, his manner more

confident, than I remembered. Apparently, Caitlin's society had had a salutary effect . . .

"Miss Hamilton?"

"Uh –" I had omitted Lady Margaret's petty efforts to drive me away, Sean's inexplicable offer of a position. But they were irrelevant. "Everything."

He adjusted his spectacles again and leaned back. "You've nothing to fear, Miss Hamilton. Neither Lady Margaret nor Miss Ashworth can hope to be appointed Mercy's legal guardian."

"Well, that's a relief."

"Nor, for that matter, can you."

"I beg your pardon? I'm afraid I don't understand."

"There is no indication that Mercy is an orphan. Or an abandoned child. Your sister has been absent, what, two weeks?"

"Going on three."

"Three weeks. I shouldn't wish to initiate action in under six months' time."

"Six months!"

"Unless you have evidence that Mrs. Ashworth will not return. A letter of farewell?" I shook my head. "Some intimation that she is – dead?"

"Nothing," I said feebly.

"Then there is no imminent question of a guardian."

"So what am I to do?" I demanded.

"First allow me to procure a copy of the will. I shall advise you if there are any conditions of residence."

"And if there aren't?"

"I can't make that decision, Miss Hamilton," he chided. "If you sincerely believe Lady Margaret intends to pilfer the child's inheritance, you should obviously remain at Ashwood. Otherwise" – he spread his bony hands – "London? America? In any event, I should be honored to serve as your solicitor."

London? America? Did he see me as one of Mr. Parker's gold mines?

"I've detained you long enough," I said stiffly. "I shall summon a carriage."

He looked wounded, and I was instantly remorseful. He had not made the law; he had traveled all the way from London . . .

"Please quote me a fee, Mr. Chapman. I haven't much cash, but –"

"Nonsense. I'll accept a favor though."

"And what is that?"

"Please extend Miss Ashworth my warmest regards."

He smiled and took my hand, and I reflected that he was, in his own way, attractive, strong.

"I'm certain Miss Ashworth would be

delighted for you to call on her," I said impulsively.

"Yes? Well. Umm."

We walked together to the stable, and I had no premonition of the terrible circumstances under which Giles Chapman and I were to meet again.

Sean and Glynis were already seated when I came down for dinner, the latter peevishly drumming her long fingernails on the tablecloth. I murmured an apology and slipped into my chair.

"I understand you had a mishap this morning," Sean said after the soup had been served. "Alf tried to tell me about it, but the poor fellow was exceedingly vague. A wheel, was it?"

"Yes, a wheel." I repeated the explanation I had given Alice's groom.

"Well, it's fortunate no one was injured."

"Exactly as I told Caitlin earlier." I nodded at the empty place across the table. "Where is Caitlin? Is she ill?"

"So she says." Glynis rang for the second course. "Nothing physical, I daresay. Caitlin has been uncommonly tiresome in recent weeks. A bundle of nerves . . ."

After dinner I went into the garden. The moon was full, but there were tattered clouds overhead, and the statues loomed up and vanished like so many silver sentries. I wandered toward Zeus, contemplating my predicament.

Without Lady Margaret's settlement I could not provide an adequate home for Mercy. She must, for the present at least, remain at Ashwood; that much was certain. And myself? Whether or not my suspicions of Lady Margaret were valid, I could scarcely abandon the child to her dubious mercies and venture forth to seek my fortune. So was I to ensconce myself at Ashwood as a poor relation, subsisting on the Ashworths' charity? Unthinkable, and there was but one alternative: I must become Mercy's governess.

The king of the gods was in shadow when I reached him. I gazed into his darkened face and massaged my shoulder, which was badly bruised and had begun to stiffen.

"*Were* you injured then, Linnet?"

"Must you always read my mind?"

"Do you find it objectionable?"

Did I? "It's rather like undressing before a lighted window."

"An interesting prospect, that."

Sean laughed, and I turned away, my cheeks blazing. He gently probed my shoulder.

"Do you need a doctor?"

"No." His touch was strangely comforting, strangely disturbing, and I drew back.

Sean inscribed a rough circle in the gravel with the toe of one boot. "Alf mentioned you had a visitor today." His voice was altogether too casual. "A gentleman from London, he thought, but then Alf does tend to get enormously confused."

I saw no reason to dissemble. "As it happens, Alf was right. I wrote my uncle's solicitor several days ago, and he was kind enough to journey down for a conference."

"A solicitor? Do you plan some sort of legal action?"

"Not immediately. I wanted to consult him about Lady Margaret's offer."

"And what was his advice?"

"That the matter is presently out of my hands. I cannot act for Mercy. Nor," I added pointedly, "can anyone else."

"I presume she will stay at Ashwood then?"

"Yes."

"Ah." A sigh of relief? "And you? Have you considered my proposition?"

"That and a number of other factors. I shan't leave Mercy here alone. However, I know nothing of governessing –"

"And when did that become a requirement of the position?" Sean chuckled. "I remember a governess of mine in particular – Miss

147

Beamer? Miss Cramer? An older woman . . ."

He went on to relate a prank he had played on the hapless spinster, and I inwardly cringed. Was this to be my fate? Perhaps Sean and Glynis would marry, and a generation hence their children would spin hilarious tales of Miss Hamilton . . .

"There is a question of supplies," I snapped, interrupting his denouement.

"Supplies? Supplies." He waved a careless hand. "We shall worry about that next week. I expect you'll find a trove of ancient treasures in the schoolroom. It's on the third floor, and I'm sure Miss Abbott has the key. Yes, with the addition of a few modern textbooks . . ."

He expounded an appropriate curriculum, but I paid him scant attention. It is done, Father. I have returned to England and assumed my rightful place. In due course I hope to meet a "suitable prospect." A coachman, a butler; or maybe I should follow up my introduction to Rodman Thatcher . . .

"Linnet?"

The moon had escaped a racing cloud, and Sean's eyes glittered in the sudden flood of light.

"Yes?"

"Apparently I've offended you in some way. I'm sorry for that."

My laugh was harsh. "There's nothing

to be sorry for." I hesitated. "I'm curious though."

"About what?"

"It was worth a great deal to Lady Margaret to be rid of us. Yet you wished us to remain. Why?"

"You haven't guessed?"

We stared at one another; for an eerie moment it seemed that he, like Zeus behind us, had turned to stone. Then Sean stepped forward and blotted out the moon.

It was not unlike Ben Tyler's kiss; not unlike, but all different. I felt a stab of pain in my shoulder as my arms crept around Sean's neck, heard the frantic din of my heart in my ears. And then, as his fingers tangled in my hair, a whisper of warning. Was this what he had intended from the beginning? He had made me his governess; was I also to be his toy? His "very good friend"?

I wrenched away, and he grunted with surprise as I darted past him. I pounded up the gravel path, gasping for breath. I glanced up once to get my bearings and thought a shadow flitted across one window of the picture gallery. But it made no difference; whatever lay ahead of me could not be half so dangerous as the spell of that moonlit garden.

EIGHT

I encountered Mary on the landing as I descended the stairs to breakfast the following morning. She was carrying a tray and bobbed her head in greeting.

"Good morning, Miss Hamilton."

"Good morning, Mary. I'm happy to see you've recovered from your illness."

"Thank you, miss."

She lifted her head, and I observed that she still appeared most unwell: she was pale, and the tray was visibly trembling in her hands. Evidently, she did not have access to the services of Alice's remarkable shaman.

"Ought you to be up?" I said kindly. "I can look after Miss Mercy if necessary —"

"No! No, thank you. Lady Margaret insisted you not be bothered. If you'll pardon me, miss —"

She trudged on up the steps, and I frowned after her. Apparently, Lady Margaret had not yet learned of my arrangement with Sean, did not realize she had lost the first round. No. She would have tossed Mercy squarely in my lap. . . . I shrugged and continued down the stairs.

Sean and Glynis were already eating; Caitlin was again absent. I had little appetite and took a scant serving of eggs and a single scone.

"Is Caitlin no better?" I asked, settling myself at the table. I directed my inquiry to Glynis, studiedly avoiding Sean's eyes.

"I wouldn't know," Glynis snapped. "Caitlin does not confide in me. She instructed Mrs. Abbott to have breakfast sent to her room."

Glynis was, even relatively, in rare ill humor. I picked at my food in silence and, as soon as I decently could, pushed my plate away and murmured excuses.

I went into the picture gallery and poked idly around. I had found it empty the night before – showing no trace of recent intrusion – and except for the legions of Ashworths staring down from the walls, it was deserted this morning as well. So whose shadow had I seen as I fled up the path? One of the servants, belatedly tidying up? Mercy's ducal ghost? Probably no shadow at all; probably a figment of my unsettled imagination.

I glanced out the nearest window. Mary and Mercy were engaged in a one-sided game of tag – Mercy scampering from tree to tree, Mary tottering weakly behind her. The poor girl could not survive the day, and I resolved – Lady Margaret's directive notwithstanding

– to relieve her after lunch.

Which left another endless morning. I could begin my inspection of the schoolroom, but Sean had reserved that for next week. . . . Sean. The whole dismal situation set me to thinking of Clara. Odd that I regarded her now with nostalgia, empathy, grudging affection. I decided impulsively to write her.

The door of my room was securely closed, and I do not know which of us was more surprised – I, frozen in the corridor, or Glynis, stationed on the Turkish rug, boldly surveying the room. I recovered first.

"Well, Glynis." I stepped inside and shut the door behind me. "An unexpected pleasure."

"Yes," she said smoothly, "I meant to mention it at breakfast. I'm lending a hand with the laundry, and if you could but point the way to your basket –"

"Has Rose been dismissed then?"

"No, but she's ill." Glynis sighed. "This absurd infection is so very tiresome. How fortunate that you have escaped." She gave me a brittle smile.

Glynis Ashworth, industriously collecting the household's dirty drawers? I suppressed a snort and experienced a flash of the intuition that Father had always attributed to my Irish heritage.

"You dropped in once before and packed up my portmanteau," I said. "What did you have in mind this time? Vandalism? Theft?"

Her green eyes narrowed, glittered with malice. "I'm not sure."

"Lady Margaret issued no specific instructions?"

"Lady Margaret had nothing to do with it."

"You took it upon yourself to drive me away?"

"Yes, I took it upon myself." Her characteristic shrillness was edged with hysteria. "And I would do it again. You and that insufferable child –"

"Mercy?"

"Mercy!" She spat it out. "She's been an affront to me since the day she was born. Edward and his outlandish will –" She began to pace the rug. "You didn't know him, Linnet. You didn't know that weak, insipid caricature of a man. You can't conceive the sacrifice I made – no, that isn't fair." She was talking half to herself. "It was a gamble: my body for Ashwood. The odds were in my favor; all I needed was a child. But Edward couldn't give me even that."

She stopped and looked again at me. "Instead there was Mercy, drooling on the furniture, mocking me ... Eventually I persuaded Edward to ban her from the house. Her and, by association, your sister, who wouldn't come without her. But he refused to change his will, refused until the very end, and then it was too late. . . ." She sucked in her breath and clenched her fists with ancient fury.

"And still is," I said levelly. "Edward's will can't be undone, Glynis. You've nothing to gain if we leave Ashwood –"

"But you have a great deal to gain by remaining, don't you?" she interrupted nastily.

"I?"

"Yes. It would make for a nice bit of insurance, wouldn't it, if you could ensnare Sean? Don't deny you've tried. I've noticed the way you look at him. I've stood in the picture gallery and watched your intimate little chats in the garden. Did I say 'chats'? It progressed considerably beyond the conversational stage last night, didn't it? Well, understand one thing, Linnet: I will not be robbed of my destiny again."

If she had misread my motives, she had deduced my emotions all too accurately, and it unnerved me to learn I was so transparent. I took refuge in sarcasm.

"Am I to infer that your destiny is to marry Sean Carlisle?"

"My destiny is to be mistress of Ashwood."

"Mercy is mistress of Ashwood," I reminded her tartly.

"Not really. Not for years. Many, many years. And fate can be so unkind. Who knows what misfortune might befall poor Mercy before she reaches her majority? Illness, a tragic accident . . ."

I felt a stir of uneasiness. "And if there *were* a – a misfortune? What would happen to Ashwood then?"

"It would revert to Sean of course. Not that I'm counting on that. Fourteen years will see me into middle age, the world into a new century. I shall settle for that. That but nothing less; and if you continue to interfere, I promise you will regret it."

She slipped past me and through the door, and I stared after her. Three games in progress then, and I was a pawn in each. And pawns, I recalled from Father's introductory chess lesson, were wonderfully expendable.

I retrieved my stationery from the chest of drawers, sat in the armchair, and started my letter to Clara. I was about halfway through a highly fictionalized account of my sojourn in England when a piercing shriek reverberated down the corridor. I leaped to my feet, scattering papers in every direction, and raced down the hall to Mercy's room, from which vicinity the cry had come. I found the child

155

collapsed against the door-jamb, alternately sniffling and wailing.

"What is it, Mercy?" I knelt beside her, examined her huddled little form, detected no gaping wounds. "Are you sick, dear?"

"Ohhh!" she wailed.

"Are you ill?" I repeated. "Does your stomach hurt?"

"No," she sniffled.

"You fell then. Did you scrape your knee?"

"It isn't me," she moaned. "It's Victoria."

"Ah." I had long recognized the possibility of Victoria's early demise. I stood and patted Mercy's shining black curls. "Well, perhaps we can fix her, dear," I said soothingly. "Let's have a look –"

"She isn't broken, Aunt Linnet. She's gone."

"Gone?"

"Yes. I left her on the chair" – Mercy pointed to the miniature rocker beneath the window – "and when I came back, she was gone."

"Maybe she fell off. Have you searched around?"

"No."

We fairly turned the room inside out. I combed the wardrobe and chest of drawers, while Mercy crawled behind the drapes and under the furniture, forgetting to cry in the excitement of the chase. But Victoria eluded us.

"She isn't here." Mercy's lips began to quiver again.

"Then I expect you took her outside and dropped her. Or put her under a nice tree in the garden –"

"I didn't take her outside."

"Are you sure, Mercy? You take Victoria everywhere –"

"Not today." She shook her head. "I was going to, but Mary said we were to play tag, and I should leave Victoria here. Mary was afraid we'd step on her. And now – now –" She broke into a fit of sobbing.

"We shall get another doll," I said, cradling her against me.

"There'll never be another Victoria."

"No, there won't. So we shall name her something altogether different. We'll give her an American name. Pocahontas."

"That's a terrible name."

"Pocahontas was an Indian."

"An Indian?" A glimmer of interest.

"Yes, a heroine."

I related the saga, which had been one of Clara's favorites. By the time Mary arrived with Mercy's lunch, the child was demanding that we obtain a genuine Indian costume from my "friends in America," and I feared I had assuaged her grief rather too well.

I returned to my room and gazed absently at the strewn stationery. Obviously, Lady Margaret had arranged to have Victoria stolen. Had instructed Mary to be certain the doll was left in Mercy's room, had dispatched someone (Caitlin?) to spirit her off. A new and marvelously vicious strategy.

And, perhaps, a winning one. I could not combat Lady Margaret if Mercy was to be her hostage.

Caitlin emerged from her seclusion on Sunday; she, along with Glynis and Sean, was seated in the landau when Mercy and I reached the drive.

"I'm glad to see you up and about, Caitlin," I said as Alf clucked the horses to a start.

"Umm," she mumbled, staring resolutely at her feet.

"Mr. Chapman wished me to extend his regards."

"Umm." I thought she blushed, though it was difficult to tell.

"Who is Mr. Chapman?" Glynis demanded.

"A gentleman from London," I said with calculated vagueness. It would do no harm for Glynis to believe that Caitlin had a suitor.

We trotted on for a moment in silence.

"I wish Victoria were here," Mercy whined at last.

"Where is Victoria?" Sean asked.

"She's been —"

"Lost," I interrupted quickly. "We can't imagine how." I glanced sideways at Caitlin, but she was seemingly transfixed by the toes of her shoes. "However, we shall purchase another doll as soon as we can."

"Better yet, let's find Mercy a family heirloom," Sean said. "I'm sure you had dolls, Caitlin. Would they be in the nursery?"

"I suppose so," she murmured.

"Why don't you take a look tomorrow, Linnet? The nursery is just off the schoolroom, as I recall."

The service was uneventful, the sermon uninspired. During the benediction, Mercy stage-whispered a prayer: "If Victoria is in heaven, please watch after her. And please make Pocahontas as lovely as Victoria was." A tall order, as Mr. Parker would have said; I hoped God, via Caitlin, would see fit to comply.

The Hineses — father and son — were deep in conversation when I came out of the sanctuary. Hines appeared uncharacteristically animated. And nervous? Colin's eyes circled the churchyard once and grazed mine, and I forced a polite smile. But

159

he, if he saw me, elected to ignore me, and I tugged Mercy to the carriage.

After breakfast the next morning I went to the kitchen to procure the schoolroom key from Mrs. Abbott. She and Hines were in the midst of a furious argument, and I lurked outside the door till he – nostrils flaring – marched past me. Mrs. Abbott stomped the floor in his wake.

"The man is impossible, Miss Hamilton. Impossible. Now it's Eliza." Eliza was one of the kitchen maids. "I'll admit the girl is clumsy" – a crash from the scullery confirmed this – "but who's to do the work if she's discharged? Not Mr. Hines, that's for certain. But he's in a terrible snit, and he's after her head. Well, that's neither here nor there, is it?" She wiped her plump hands on her apron. "Would you be wanting another scone?"

"No, thank you. I need the schoolroom key."

"The schoolroom key?" she echoed dubiously.

"You don't have it? Mr. Carlisle thought –"

"Oh, I have it all right. But Lady Margaret said no one was to go up there. It was in a frightful mess, she told me, and the maids weren't to waste their time –"

"The situation has changed, Mrs. Abbott. Evidently you haven't heard: I am now

160

Mercy's governess."

"Oh?" She tried and failed to mask her surprise. "Oh, I see. I'll send someone to tidy up then –"

"That won't be necessary. Not just yet. I'll determine what has to be done and let you know."

Mrs. Abbott took a great brass ring from a nail on the wall and fumbled through the jangling assortment of keys, jabbering directions all the while. Eventually she gave me a rusted key and I left the kitchen, unpleasantly aware of her curious eyes on my back.

The staircase, which lay at the end of the second-floor hallway, was narrow and steep, and I paused at the top for breath. The corridor bore the stamp of neglect: the wooden floor was cloaked in dust, and cobwebs adorned the walls. I proceeded to "the second door on the left, directly above your room, Miss Hamilton," and fitted my key in the lock.

The schoolroom was musty and dirty but not as cluttered as I had expected. It contained half a dozen student desks of varying sizes; a full-sized oak desk and accompanying chair, equally dilapidated; a chalk-board; a tall cabinet; an array of built-in bookshelves. I sat gingerly in the oak chair and found it remarkably uncomfortable.

I sighed and went to the cabinet. Scarcely a treasure trove; it was, except for one yellowed tablet, empty. Mercy would require a complete set of supplies. I sorted through the books, my hands growing black, and located several elementary reading and mathematics texts. Enough to begin with, no doubt. A brief trip to Leatherhead, a spate of dusting and polishing, and I could embark upon my dreary pedagogical career.

Meanwhile, there was the quest for Pocahontas. I walked toward the door in the right-hand wall, wondering if Caitlin minded Sean's casual appropriation of her dolls. She had voiced no objection, but then Caitlin was, like her late elder brother, eminently tractable.

The door was warped, and I wrested it open to expose the "frightful mess" Mrs. Abbott had warned me of. The nursery had been converted to a storeroom and a most disorderly one indeed. I stepped over a pile of drapes in front of the door and peered into the shadows beyond, my eyes gradually adjusting to the gloom. There was a wild assortment of odds and ends: a three-legged chair, disgorging its stuffings; a cracked chamber pot; a sagging étagère, groaning with wounded bric-a-brac; heaps of faded clothing, tattered

162

books, miscellaneous refuse. And nowhere, of course, a doll.

I started plowing through the debris and nearly forgot my mission. Here was a hoopskirt – Lady Margaret's? How had its wearer, whoever she was, negotiated any but the widest doorways? A battered violin, bereft of strings. A sword – did it date from the Napoleonic wars? The Crimea? A fan, once exquisite, the fabric now detached from the ribs. A single glove, encrusted with tiny pearls – had it clothed the hand that held the fan? Had its mate been lost at a glittering ball long before I was born?

I poked around for half an hour or so and then gave up; if Caitlin's dolls were about, they were hopelessly interred. I turned to go and snagged my skirt on an outcropping near the floor.

I stooped, disentangled my dress, and glanced at the impediment – a heavily carved right angle of wood. A frame? I wedged my hand between the folds of a lace tablecloth and confirmed it: a picture was lodged within the teetering stack of linens. Justin perhaps? Mildly curious, I grasped the protruding corner and began to ease the picture out.

Darkness and heat descended together, and I later remember thinking that one of the tablecloths had slipped off the pile and over

163

my head. I struggled to free myself, and there was a jerk, and I lost my precarious balance and thudded to the floor. I clawed at my silken prison, dimly aware of the sounds beyond: shallow breathing, ripping fabric, rapid footsteps. Silence.

I had always had an irrational fear of confinement, and I blinked back tears of panic. I was doomed to die here, to suffocate.... At last my frantic fingers found wood, and I wrenched my shroud away, gulping great lungfuls of air as I emerged into the light.

I stood up and gazed around the nursery, my heart still hammering against my ribs. The topmost curtain from the heap before the door – I had remarked its peculiar pinkish hue – now lay at my feet. The linen mountain was dangerously atilt, and a ragged ladder of lace spilled partway down its side. And the picture was gone.

I hurried out of the nursery and the schoolroom, pausing only to lock the door. Glynis, I decided, as I sped down the hall. Glynis had known I would visit the nursery today. Glynis had stalked me, seized her opportunity, thrown that loathsome drapery over my head. Grabbed the picture, shredding the lace tablecloth in the process. But why? I rushed into my room and collapsed against the door. Why take the picture?

I couldn't guess, and I elected not to pursue it. I did not want Glynis to know how badly she had frightened me. When, at dinner, Sean inquired about my exploration of the schoolroom, Glynis maintained an expression of perfect innocence.

"The textbooks are adequate," I said, "but we shall need a whole raft of supplies. Tablets, pens, chalk –"

"Make a list," Sean said carelessly, "and we'll drive into Leatherhead later in the week. You haven't seen the town yet, have you? We'll tour around a bit –"

"What fun!" Glynis interjected. "And how convenient. I have some shopping to do myself. And one does like a man along to carry the parcels, doesn't one, Linnet?"

She flashed a smug smile, and I silently conceded her the second score of the day.

Alice waylaid me just after breakfast Tuesday morning.

"You'll never guess what's happened, Miss Hamilton," she said, clutching my arm. Her demeanor promised nothing short of the Second Coming.

"What?"

"We're to go to Long Hill Farm," she said triumphantly.

"Oh?"

"A stroke of fortune it was, miss. Mrs. Abbott has put up some plum preserves, and she chanced to mention it to Mr. Carlisle, and *he* chanced to remember that plum preserves are a special favorite of Mr. Hines. Mr. Colin Hines, that is. So they decided – Mr. Carlisle and Mrs. Abbott – that I should take some over to Long Hill Farm." She glanced at the grandfather clock. "Perhaps we ought to leave at once, miss."

"We? How did I become involved in this, Alice?"

"It was Mr. Carlisle's idea. When I told him I couldn't handle a rig, he suggested you drive me. He seemed to think you'd enjoy a little outing. As I'm sure you will, miss; it's a lovely day. . . ."

The gig was hitched and drawn up outside the stable, the bay mare in the traces. I inspected the errant wheel, found it securely repaired, and took the driver's seat.

The road was dry and fast, and we clipped along at a smart pace. Alice delivered an incessant monologue on her avocation: men. Her romantic adventures were so numerous and entangled that I was unable to make much sense of her narrative. "Rob," I eventually inferred, was the handsome groom with the mystic power of healing. "Jim" was the son of a tavern-keeper in Leatherhead. "Bill" was evidently her favorite, but she neglected to tell me who or where he was. "Jack" and "Harry" were described in the past tense, though Alice would "never forget Harry." There were brief references to "Tom" and "Roy," and I wondered how Alice proposed to accommodate Rodman Thatcher in her hectic schedule.

The farmhouse drive was a mile or so beyond the field where I had stopped on my previous visit. We turned in, and Alice began patting her hair, pinching her cheeks and biting color into her lips. By the time I reined the horse in, she was fairly quivering with anticipation.

The drive expired in a rough circle surrounded by buildings: the house – a sturdy, unprepossessing stone dwelling; a small stone structure that I assumed to be the dairy; a ramshackle chicken house; a toolshed; a barn. As Alice and I clambered down from the gig, a woman emerged from the dairy.

"Hello, Betsy, Alice here. We've brought some plum preserves."

Alice led me forward, handed over her basket of preserves, and performed appropriate introductions. Betsy was, as Alice had reported, singularly unattractive, and her appearance was in no way enhanced by a painful squint. Alice remarked that I had recently come down from London, and Betsy launched into an interminable account of her one trip to the city: she had attended the Great Exhibition in 1851. I murmured an occasional "Oh?" and "Yes?" while Alice, like a well-trained hunting dog, sniffed about the buildings.

Betsy was telling me, for the third time, how she had happened to glimpse the Queen when Alice spotted her quarry. She bounded toward the barn, where Rodman Thatcher lounged in the doorway, and they were soon engaged in lively conversation. I turned back to Betsy, who had, miraculously, paused for breath.

"Did you discuss the exhibition with my sister, Betsy? I know she would have been fascinated."

"Would she now?" Betsy preened. "Well, I'm sorry to say there was no chance. I was busy in the bedrooms" – she nodded toward the upper floor of the house – "and I missed Mrs. Ashworth altogether."

"You didn't even see her?"

"I don't see anything very well, Miss Hamilton." She smiled ruefully, displaying a mouthful of blackened teeth. "I heard the trap, but I couldn't make out who was calling. Later on Mr. Hines said it was Mr.

Carlisle and Mrs. Ashworth. She went to the exhibition, you say?"

"No." Her eyesight was indeed faulty. "No, though I believe my father did –"

"And did he ever mention the piano? It was the most cunning thing, Miss Hamilton – a piano that folded down to form a table . . ."

She rattled on, and I inwardly squirmed, glancing from time to time at Alice and Rodman Thatcher. I hated to interrupt their flirtation – which seemed to be progressing very nicely – but I doubted I could survive Betsy's apparently endless reminiscences. I was casting about for another topic – any other topic – when there was a thunder of hoofbeats in the drive.

"What the devil is going on here?" Colin Hines roared.

He jerked the gray horse to a hard halt, and the animal reared, nearly – to my keen satisfaction – spilling Mr. Hines in the dust. He steadied the horse, dismounted, and stood, arms akimbo, eyes darting furiously from barn to dairy and back.

"What the devil is going on?" he repeated louder, if possible, than before. "How many times must I warn you, Thatcher? Stop ogling that – that young woman and get back to work."

Rodman Thatcher eyed him for a moment –

insolently? – then disappeared into the barn.

"As for you –"

But Betsy was already slinking toward the dairy, and he let her go. Alice had plastered herself against the barn – evidently seeking invisibility – and Colin Hines directed his attention to me.

"I do apologize, Miss Hamilton." He whipped another disgraceful handkerchief from his pocket and mopped his streaming face. "I –"

"As well you should," I interrupted coldly, my temper at a dangerous simmer. "We brought some plum preserves, and I'm frankly inclined to take them back. We've been here but a few minutes, and I can't suppose we've done any irreparable harm. If we have, please understand that the fault is mine. Good day, Mr. Hines."

I signaled Alice and stalked regally to the gig. Alice leaped in beside me. As we tore down the drive, Alice muttered under her breath and I urged the mare to feats of speed she had long since forgotten. I slowed down only after we were well along the road, and Alice simultaneously found her tongue.

"Well, I never," she sniffed indignantly. "The nerve of him, Miss Hamilton. Rodman said he was a perfect bas – that he was hard to work for, but he's such a good-*looking* man.

But then looks aren't everything, are they? Now Rodman, Rodman is a gentleman. Do you think he could be the younger son of a duke or some such? He has a fancy air about him."

Alice continued to prattle about Rodman Thatcher, but I paid her scant attention. Colin Hines was overdue for a comeuppance, I reflected grimly. He might be "fearfully bright," but he was nevertheless a butler's son ... And I a Coachman's Daughter, and Rodman Thatcher, perhaps, a cut above us both. It becomes very complicated, doesn't it, Father?

Rob (or was it Roy?) was waiting at the stable to hand Alice out of the trap. She greeted him with distinct coolness, and I guessed his days, like Jack's and Harry's before him, were numbered. I descended unassisted from the gig and went to the house.

It was not yet eleven, and I glowered at the grandfather clock, as though it were responsible for its sluggish hands. I wandered into the garden, thinking to join Mercy and Mary in one of their manifold entertainments.

But the garden was deserted, and I supposed they were all – Mary, Mercy, and the gardeners as well – at lunch. I had turned to go inside when I sensed a flaw in the scene and turned back. The statues gleamed pristinely in the sunlight, the hedges were immaculately trimmed . . . The bridge. I walked a few yards down the path and shaded my eyes. There was a gap in the footbridge that led from the lakeshore to the island; evidently Sean had misjudged its strength. I should barricade the landward end, I thought, lest Mercy . . .

Mercy! I cannot say what it was that triggered a thrill of apprehension, but I found myself racing down the path, my eyes sweeping the placid blue water beneath the bridge. I saw her just as I reached the shore – a thrashing bundle of white fabric and black hair.

"Mercy!" I screamed.

"Aunt Linnet!"

She waved her arms, then sank, with awful grace, below the surface.

NINE

I was later to marvel at the mind's agility in a moment of crisis. How deep was the water? I wondered. Clearly over Mercy's head; over mine as well? Father had taught me to swim in the creek behind Hamilton Oaks, but that had been years before, and he had remained but a few feet away, frequently assisting my clumsy efforts. Did I remember the strokes at all? And what of my clothes; would they not drag me down? All this within a split second, and then Mercy surfaced again, spewing forth a small fountain of water.

I tore off my shoes and waded into the lake, muttering an incoherent prayer. The water reached my knees, my waist, and I fought the sodden weight of my skirt and petticoats. To the top of my rib cage now; dear God, how much farther? Where was she?

The water was lapping at my shoulders when she bobbed up not half a yard in front of me. I lunged for one flailing arm but got her hair instead, and she – to my inexpressible relief – yelped with pain. I drew her toward me and hooked my fingers under the collar of her dress.

"I'm going to pull you in now," I said calmly. "Just lie back on the water."

"Victoria," she gasped.

"Hush, Mercy! Don't say another word!"

Gulping agonizingly for breath, I dragged a coughing, sputtering Mercy back the way I had come. We attained the shore at last, and I picked her up, staggered, and set her abruptly in the mud. I collapsed beside her, trembling with exhaustion and belated panic.

"Are you all right, dear?" I wheezed at length.

"Yes." She had, in fact, weathered the experience considerably better than I. "But we must rescue Victoria."

"Victoria?" I croaked absently.

"I found her, Aunt Linnet! You see, she's on the island."

She pointed, her slender little arm nakedly exposed under the wet transparency of her sleeve. I sighted along her finger and eventually perceived a slash of red on the steps of the temple – Victoria in the most regal of her several costumes. I suppose I was too drained to question the doll's miraculous reappearance.

"So she is," I said mildly, my respiration slowing toward normal.

"Well, we can't just leave her there," Mercy said huffily. "Victoria's afraid of the dark. I was going to get her when the bridge broke –"

She chattered on, but I scarcely heard her. I had begun to recover, and I felt a vague prickle of alarm.

"You saw Victoria on the island?" I interrupted her commentary.

"Yes." With labored patience.

"And you started across the bridge, and the bridge gave way –"

"And I fell in the lake. And how are we

174

to reach Victoria now? The bridge is gone —" Moist black eyes; a flicker of hope. "But you can swim, Aunt Linnet! You can swim right out and bring her back."

"Where was Mary when you noticed Victoria?"

"Inside."

"Why inside?"

"She had an errand. You *are* going to save Victoria, aren't you?"

"What kind of errand?"

"I don't know," she said fretfully. "We came out and decided to play hide-and-seek. We walked down to that big rock on the shore — that's our starting point — and Mary said she had an errand she'd forgotten. She told me to look for a good hiding place. Then she went in, and I did look, and I saw Victoria. She could *die*, you know, if you don't go after her."

"Someone will go after her; I promise you that." I struggled to my feet and tugged Mercy up behind me. "Meanwhile, you need a nap."

"I'm not tired," she whined, sagging against me to belie her protest. "I'm worried about Victoria . . ."

Mrs. Abbott — with the servant's unerring nose for drama — was bustling into the picture gallery as we entered.

"Miss Hamilton!" She gawked at my soggy raiment. "Miss Mercy! A swim, was it? I've heard tell of folks bathing without a stitch on –"

"Mercy fell in the lake, Mrs. Abbott. Fortunately, she wasn't injured, and if you could help her to her room –"

Actually, it took both of us to maneuver the child up the stairs; she was, by now, almost asleep on her feet. I left Mrs. Abbott to put her to bed, tottered to my own room, and wearily stripped off my soaked clothing. Mary would have an explanation, I thought, donning my dressing gown. Mary *must* have an explanation; my dark, almost formless suspicion could not possibly be true. . . .

"Ah, you're headed for a nap as well then." Mrs. Abbott barged unceremoniously through the door. "And a good thing it is. Would you be wanting a cup of tea before? It's not likely you'll catch cold, what with the day so warm –"

"I wish to see Mary, Mrs. Abbott."

"Umm." She frowned. "It's a bit tricky, isn't it, miss? I'm not denying the girl behaved in a most irresponsible manner, but she *is* Lady Margaret's personal maid –"

"I know my place, Mrs. Abbott!" I snapped. "I shan't discharge her." She looked wounded, and I bit my lip in mute

176

apology. "I hoped she'd be able to shed some light on the mishap."

"Of course, miss," she murmured. "I'll send her right up."

I sank into the armchair, my muscles beginning to throb, and studiedly blanked my mind. I would not speculate; I would hear Mary out. . . .

"Well, if that isn't the most outrageous thing!"

Mrs. Abbott's voice penetrated my uneasy doze, and I shook myself awake and focused on the plump, black figure in the doorway.

"The most outrageous thing," she repeated indignantly. "I hardly know how to tell you this, Miss Hamilton: Mary is gone."

"Gone?" I echoed sharply, fully alert.

"Gone. I looked everywhere for her, even knocked up Lady Margaret – Mr. Hines will have a field day with *that*, I can tell you – but she was nowhere to be found. So I went up to her room – the girl *has* been ill, after all – but she wasn't there. Well, on an off-chance – call it a hunch, miss – I glanced in the wardrobe, and it was quite empty. She must have packed up and left without a word to anyone. I expect she guessed she'd be royally read out. Except –"

"Except what?"

"Nothing, miss." She shook her head. "I
177

shudder to think what Mr. Hines is going to say. Are you sure you wouldn't care for a cup of tea?"

"No, thank you. That will be all, Mrs. Abbott."

She went out, wringing her hands, no doubt rehearsing her confrontation with Hines. I gazed sightlessly at the closed door, wondering at her "except." Did Mrs. Abbott share my reservations about Mary's abrupt departure?

It made superficial sense. Mary had shirked her duties, had provoked a near tragedy, had run off before she could be summarily dismissed. Except ... Except there hadn't been enough time. Mercy could have been in the water a minute or two at most when I spotted her. The seemingly interminable rescue had required but a few minutes more. Our conversation on the shore, the journey up the stairs – another ten. And five minutes later Mrs. Abbott had initiated her search. Twenty minutes then. Within twenty minutes Mary had left Mercy, performed her errand, returned to the garden, realized the enormity of her lapse, packed, and disappeared. And how had she managed the latter feat? Was she even now trudging along the road to Leatherhead, gripping a battered valise with all her worldly goods inside?

It was remotely possible, I admitted. If Mercy had started across the bridge just as Mary came back to the garden; if Mary had seen her fall, had fled at once to her room, packed ... Except it wasn't in character. Mary would not have abandoned the child to that watery grave. She would have attempted to save her or, barring that, would have sought help. And I would have encountered her floundering in the lake or shrieking through the house.

Which meant the incident had been carefully planned. With Mary's participation? I thought not; I thought Mary was, no less than I, a pawn. She had abetted Victoria's kidnapping all unknowing, never dreaming the doll's ultimate mission. And, still unknowing, had been removed – hustled into a waiting trap, driven from Ashwood to a "better position." A position in a remote county where she'd be unlikely to learn of Mercy's, Mercy's ...

Death! I silently hissed. Death. Someone was trying to kill Mercy, and he or she had tried before. The accident in the gig had not been an accident. Caitlin had realized it; I remembered her unwonted hysteria. Caitlin had warned me of danger long ago, that first night at Ashwood ...

So was Caitlin involved in the plot? I

could not believe it. Caitlin cowered in a figurative corner, observing the world through her rimless spectacles, drawing her terrible conclusions, lacking the courage to voice them. Caitlin had hinted; would – could – do no more. And how did Caitlin stand to benefit by Mercy's death?

Lady Margaret then. Glynis. Both had wished Mercy gone ... Gone. Safe. Only Sean had insisted we stay. Why? Because Mercy was all that stood between him and Ashwood. Because he could not hope to kill her on a busy London street ...

I strove frantically to disprove my theory, but the pieces clicked inexorably into place. When had Sean first asked me to remain at Ashwood? Just after I had broached the possibility of selling the estate. A few days later the wheel had flown off the gig; Sean, I recalled, had seen to the hitching of the trap. Giles Chapman had arrived that very afternoon, and Sean had been exceedingly curious about the legal ramifications of his visit. I had agreed to stay on, and Sean had been visibly relieved, had tossed in a bit of romance to reinforce my decision. Then Victoria had vanished; why had I assumed Lady Margaret to be responsible? Sean was master of Ashwood and could order the servants about as he pleased. He had been grandly unconcerned about the procurement of supplies for the schoolroom; had he known Mercy would not live to be educated? This morning, conveniently forgetting Colin Hines's historic "touchiness," he had sent me blithely off to Long Hill Farm. Had planted Victoria on the island, had sawed through the bridge – which he had proclaimed "quite safe" – had dispatched Mary to parts unknown . . .

My first inclination was to flee. To leave my – Mercy's – sodden clothes where they lay and board the next train to London. Aunt Jane could not, under the circumstances, refuse to take us in. . . . But would Aunt Jane believe me? She was a thoroughly pragmatic woman, and I hadn't a shred of proof. The wheel *could* have fallen off the gig; such mishaps occurred every day. Mercy *could* have left Victoria on the steps of the temple. The bridge *could* have collapsed by accident. If I flounced out of Ashwood and Aunt Jane turned us away, Mercy and I could not long survive on my slender resources . . .

There was a knock at the door, and I heaved myself out of my chair and opened it.

"Are you all right?" Sean said.

His eyes flickered over me, and I briefly regretted my immodest attire, then shrugged the thought aside. In view of all that had, or might have, passed between us, my dishabille was trifling indeed.

"Yes, I'm all right. Mercy is as well," I added pointedly.

"So I understand. May I come in?" Rhetorical – he shouldered his way past me and closed the door. "Mrs. Abbott seemed to feel it was touch and go however."

I shall never know whether I had intended to keep my suspicions to myself. As it was, something within me lashed out at that casual remark: anger, fear, ravaged expectations – something.

"It was indeed. It was Colin Hines who crossed you up, Sean."

"Crossed me up?"

"You should have remembered how difficult he can be. How rude. If he'd mustered a single pleasantry, it would have been too late. I'd have lingered at Long Hill Farm for ten minutes, half an hour – but a second or two would have been sufficient, wouldn't it?"

"What the devil are you talking about?"

"Mercy would be dead, wouldn't she? Father – Stevens, is it? – would be here by now, and we'd be planning the funeral. A child's funeral; uniquely sad. Father Stevens might ask about a special, precious toy. But Victoria would be long gone –"

"Linnet –"

"The gig accident was easier by half, wasn't it? Once you got past Alf and loosened the wheel. . . . This time you had too many characters to manipulate, Sean. Most unfortunate because I shan't give you another chance."

"Another chance? Good God, Linnet, do you believe I'm trying to kill Mercy?"

"What would you have me believe? That Victoria was breathed to life by a fairy godmother and strolled out to the island unassisted?"

"Has it not occurred to you that Mercy left her there? The child's only seven –"

"Ah. The tale you concocted for the constable. In the event you couldn't dispose of Victoria before he arrived. Well, I'm not the constable, Sean. There have been two attempts on Mercy's life, and who else has a reason to kill her? Answer me that. Who else?"

His eyes narrowed, but he said nothing, and I pressed my advantage.

"I asked once why you wished us to remain at Ashwood. Now I know."

"No, you don't, my dear," he said levelly. "You didn't know then, and you don't know now. I asked you to stay at Ashwood because I love you."

He moved with the swiftness and grace of

an animal, reached me before I realized what he was about, caught me in an embrace I could not have escaped had I wanted to. And I did not want to; that was the astonishing part. Whatever he was, whatever he had done, I loved him, had from the start; and for a moment I reveled in the warmth of him, the smell, gave myself up to the hard, searching mouth on mine. Then, as I had on that night in the garden, I tore away, backed to the wall, and cringed there, my arms outstretched as though physically to ward him off.

"I shan't attack you, Linnet," he said coldly, a catch in his voice.

"No, violence is best reserved for children, isn't it?" My bitterness was mostly for my own weakness, my shattered dreams.

"Oh, God." He ran his fingers through his black hair, recovered himself. "What do you intend to do?"

Oddly enough, the encounter – like a cautery – had purged my muddled mind. "I'm not going to the police; you can rest easy on that account. The evidence is far too circumstantial for me to bring charges. Which I'm sure you anticipated. No, Mercy and I shall travel up to London tomorrow, and I shall confer with Mr. Chapman. I expect he'll recommend a civil suit. With Ashwood so poorly administered that Mercy's very life is in constant danger –" I endeavored a sarcastic smile, failed. "I shall sleep in Mercy's room tonight. I don't think you're sufficiently rash to stage another attempt so hard on the heels of the last, but I shan't risk it."

"As you wish," he said politely. "Is there any way I can assist you?"

"As a matter of fact, there is. I promised Mercy Victoria would be returned to her. And as you've no doubt recovered the doll –" Another abortive smile. "Just give her to Alice. I assume Alice is in charge of Mercy, now you've sent Mary away?"

His eyes slitted again, but he turned and left without a further word.

My insistence on sleeping in Mercy's room was merely a gesture; I did not suppose for an instant that Sean would hazard another assault that day. My confidence was such that I collapsed on the bed and dozed through the afternoon, tormented by dreams I was never able to reconstruct. Alice knocked me up with an early dinner, which I did not want and could not eat.

"How peculiar about Mary," she mused, unloading the tray on the bedside cabinet.

"Most peculiar," I agreed. Then, with a flash of intuition: "Did Mary discuss her plans with you, Alice?"

185

"No, miss, she didn't. Though she did say" – Alice stopped and fumbled gratuitously with the napkin and silverware.

"Said what?"

"That there was something very odd afoot. But I took it with a grain of salt. Mary was always talking of ghosts and mermen and werewolves –"

She rattled on; was she hiding something? If so, I lacked the energy to draw her out. I began to pick at the boiled chicken, and Alice lapsed into silence, hovering – unusually attentive – at my elbow.

"Did anyone mention I'm to stay in Miss Mercy's room tonight?" I asked at last.

"Yes, Mr. Carlisle told me to fix up a bed. Do you think the poor little lass'll have nightmares then?"

"Umm," I grunted noncommittally.

"Well, Mrs. Abbott found a cot. It isn't much, and I fear you won't sleep a wink. But it's all made up and turned down –" She glowered at my almost untouched plate.

"And did you take Victoria to Miss Mercy?"

"Victoria?"

"Her doll."

"Oh, yes, Mr. Carlisle mentioned that as well. He said to tell you the doll had disappeared."

"Disappeared?" I repeated incredulously.

"Yes. He went out to the island, he said, and 'the doll has disappeared.' His exact words, miss." Her eyes sparked with peasant cunning. "Was it valuable?"

"Only to Miss Mercy." Why? I wondered wildly. It made no sense at all; Victoria was dead bait . . .

"Are you finished, miss?" I had consumed no more than half a dozen bites, but it was a lost cause, and I nodded. "I'll just light the lamp then –"

"It's still broad daylight, Alice," I protested.

"So it is. But I have an engagement this evening, and I'm in a bit of a hurry –"

"Rob?" I asked. "Or –" But the rest of them escaped me.

"I'm afraid it's a secret, miss," Alice said coyly. She reloaded the tray with an impatient clatter. "Shall I bring your bath to Miss Mercy's room tomorrow?"

"No, wake me, and I'll come back here. And don't be late, Alice. Miss Mercy and I are going up to London."

She nodded and flew out of the door, and I gazed after her. Enviously? Alice had nothing and everything, I reflected. Eventually she would marry one of her rustic suitors and settle into a life of perfect contentment while

187

I. . . . Why did it have to be you, Sean? Why did it have to be you?

Mercy's nap had wholly revived her; she was bouncing about on the cot and nearly bowled me over as she catapulted off.

"It isn't a toy, Mercy," I said sternly, eyeing the cot's dilapidated legs.

"Well, of course it isn't. It's a bed. And what is it doing in here?"

"I thought it would be fun if I slept with you tonight."

"Oh, it will, Aunt Linnet! You and I and Victoria –" She glanced at my empty hands, and her black eyes narrowed. "Where is Victoria?"

"She's been misplaced, dear."

"What does that mean?"

What indeed? "Amidst all the confusion she got lost. I'm sure she'll turn up –"

"You left her on the island! And after you promised –"

"Victoria is not on the island, Mercy."

She narrowed her eyes again, suspiciously. How quickly she was growing up, learning to trust in no one, nothing. . . . She brightened. "Maybe Mary found her. I shall go and ask –" She stopped, and I could almost hear the busy whir of her fertile mind. "Where is Mary?"

There was no easy way to tell her. "She's

left Ashwood, dear. She has a much better position, and we should be very happy for her –"

But it was too much – this dual bereavement – and Mercy burst into tears.

"I have wonderful news though." Shameless cajolery. "We're going up to London tomorrow –"

I believe I promised her a new doll, a new dress, and a ride on the underground railway. I lulled her to sleep with a story of my own devising – *Hansel and Gretel* restaged in an American Indian setting – and crawled into the cot.

It was quite as uncomfortable as Alice had suggested, and I tossed and turned and speculated. Could I possibly be wrong about Sean? Glynis had brazenly contemplated the advantages of Mercy's death – too brazenly. She wasn't likely to smack her lips at the prospect of Mercy's demise, then rush out to arrange it. And Lady Margaret had demanded from the start that we leave Ashwood.

Had I misjudged her? I suddenly wondered. Had she somehow deduced Sean's intentions? Without proof – and Sean was too clever to give her that – what could she, would she, have done? She would have attempted to send Mercy safely away, I silently answered. Failing in that, she would have assigned her personal servant to act as the child's bodyguard. She would have dredged up the wherewithal for a handsome settlement and – when her nephew uncovered her desperate financial maneuvers – would have quarreled with him. Would have tried to convince him that twenty thousand pounds was "nothing," that it was to his advantage to pick the meaty bones of the estate. . . .

So it all came back to Sean – Sean of the black hair and the laughing black eyes. Sean. Sean. . . .

I must have slept, for when the sound came I was fuzzy. I had locked the door; was someone fumbling with the knob? I lay there, my heart crashing in my ears, until I realized the noise was at the window. I crept across the room and flicked the blue curtain aside.

There was no moon, and I squinted into the darkness. Eventually I got my bearings, made out the ancient, malformed beech that stood beside the stable, then – squat and square – the stable itself. I would not have seen it had it not chosen that moment to move: a trap, subtly blacker than the night. It proceeded cautiously down the drive – a squeak here, a clop there, marking its hesitant passage. It slipped around the corner of the house and out of sight.

Alice and Rob, no doubt, daring a midnight

excursion. Exhaustion overcame me in waves, and I groped my way back to the cot.

I had no watch, and there was no clock in Mercy's room, so when I woke I had only a vague impression that it was late. The blue bedroom was too bright, and I – in view of that agonizing night on the cot – too refreshed. I stole down to my own room, glanced at the mantel clock, and erupted into fury. Half past nine! It was long since time to put an end to Alice's far-flung idylls. I yanked the bell-pull, and a few minutes later Mrs. Abbott panted through the door.

"Yes, miss?"

"Where is Alice?" I demanded.

"Alice?" Her eyes darted about as though she hoped to find Alice lurking behind the drapes. "Now that you mention it, miss, I haven't seen her this morning. I gave it no thought, figuring you'd be quite done in –"

"Never mind," I snapped. "Please wake Miss Mercy and see she's dressed in half an hour. We'll have some scones, no more. Tell Alf we'll be traveling to Leatherhead, then on to London. . . ."

I completed my instructions, splashed my face in yesterday's cold water, and seethed. Mr. Parker's democratic notions would wither and die in the English countryside. . . .

Mercy's mouth was slathered with plum preserves when I reached the dining room. I choked down a warm, butter-laden scone and began to relent. Alice had never been conspicuously dependable, and Mary's precipitous departure had no doubt plunged the household into turmoil. I decided to check on Alf before I herded Mercy out to the stable.

"Have another scone, dear," I said. "I'll fetch you when the rig is ready."

The rig was not ready. The stable – to heap insult on injury – was deserted. I stalked to the coach house, my temper bubbling out of control again. Another tidbit to pass along to Mr. Chapman.

"Alf!"

He was perched on the box of the landau, staring dreamily into space, and – to my immense, petty gratification – he jumped.

"What the devil are you doing, Alf?" Crude and wonderfully ineffective. He gazed over my head, his fingers toying with imaginary reins. "Did Mrs. Abbott not tell you we're going to London?"

"London?" he echoed dully.

"Just hitch a trap," I snarled. "Any trap. We'll take the gig and leave it at the station if we must –" I don't know what it was that caught me up. He was disoriented, but I had grown to expect that; was he troubled as well?

192

"Is something wrong, Alf?"

"It's not like the other one," he said expressionlessly.

"What's not like what other one?"

"Not like the other one."

"What's —" But it was futile. "Obviously, you're upset, Alf. You've seen something, haven't you? Perhaps you could show me, take me there —"

"Take you. Yes, I'll take you."

But not just yet. He made as if to hitch the landau, and I reminded him there were just the two of us. The brougham then? I suggested the gig, and he fumbled interminably with the harness. . . . We were ready at last, the gelding in the traces. Alf looked me a question, and I took the driver's seat, motioning him in beside me.

"Where, Alf? Where is it?"

"The road."

We trotted down the drive, and I halted at the foot. "Which direction? Left or right?"

He hesitated, waved his left hand.

I turned the horse and urged him forward. "Now you must guide me to the exact place, Alf. You do remember it, don't you?"

Maybe, maybe not. He stopped me twice, clambered out of the gig, surveyed the territory, climbed back in, and mumbled me on. How had I got myself into this? I should

193

be well on the way to London. . . .

"Stop!" he ordered.

I reined the gelding wearily in, and Alf leaped down and peered over a grassy mound at the side of the road.

"This is it," he said with relative excitement.

I clucked the horse to the next tree, got down, tied the horse, crossed the road.

"What is it, Alf?"

He pulled me up the mound and pointed. "It's not like the other one," he repeated.

How could it be? Alice lay in the shallow ditch below us. And Alice had been hacked quite to pieces.

TEN

"Dear God." I turned away, swallowing a surge of nausea. "Dear God."

"It's Alice, ain't it?" Alf said laconically.

"Yes, it's Alice. You did right to bring me here, Alf. Now you must stay, stay right here at the side of the road, and I shall summon the police. You understand, don't you? You're not to move."

"Yes'm."

I drove the horse furiously, mercilessly, back toward Ashwood, wondering why I was in such a hurry. Poor Alice was utterly beyond human help – her clothes ripped to shreds, her freckled body slashed and sliced in half a hundred places. . . . I retched again and slapped the exhausted gelding to a gallop.

Hines and Mrs. Abbott were entrenched on either side of the grandfather clock, sniping at one another. They glanced up as I tore through the front door, fell silent, and stared at me with unabashed curiosity.

"It's Alice," I panted, collapsing against the door. "Alice is – Alice has been murdered."

I could recall nothing of what came next; perhaps having discharged my responsibility, I closed my mind to the horror down the road. Mrs. Abbott later said that I behaved quite rationally – describing the scene of the crime, the condition of the corpse, the circumstances of its discovery – but I remembered none of it. When awareness returned, I was at the kitchen table sipping a cup of tea as Mrs. Abbott peered anxiously across at me.

"Alice," I mumbled.

"Mr. Hines has gone for the police," she said soothingly. "How awful for you, miss. How perfectly awful. Of course" – she sighed – "it was bound to happen. I warned the girl repeatedly. 'You're tempting fate,' I told her. 'You can't leap into bed with every man who happens by –' Pardon me, miss." She lowered her eyes.

"You think it was one of her lovers then? The – the person who killed her?"

"Who else? Unless –" she frowned, "– unless it was the gypsies again."

"Gypsies? Again?"

"It was many years ago, when Maude was at Ashwood. A most brutal murder. The body was cut to ribbons –" I sloshed a great river of tea into my saucer, and Mrs. Abbott bit her lip. "A young woman then as well. They found her – if I'm not mistaken – near where you found Alice. There was a band of gypsies camped in the neighborhood, and, well, you know gypsies. Everyone assumed one of them was responsible. The more since they disappeared that very night."

"And are there gypsies in the vicinity now?"

"Not to my knowledge, miss. But it's worth an investigation, isn't it? I shall mention it to the constable."

He arrived about noon. I had consumed innumerable cups of tea by then, and my hands and stomach were equally unsteady when Hines came to escort me to the drawing room.

Inspector Stevens was the parson's cousin

196

and had his relative's squarish jaw and thinning brown hair. The resemblance, however, died at the eyes: the priest's were brown and sympathetic; the constable's gray and chilly. He nodded me to a chair and extracted a small notebook from his coat pocket. He recorded my name and position in the household and asked me to recount Alf's and my grim mission. Then:

"When did you last see Miss Milton alive?"

Milton. I had never known Alice's surname. "Last night. About six, I guess."

"And did you discuss her plans for the evening?"

"Not in any detail. She said she had an engagement –"

"Ah." He scribbled eagerly in his notebook. "With a gentleman, I presume?"

"Yes."

"A specific gentleman?"

"Well, it would be, wouldn't it?" I snapped. I was tired and nervous and found him unaccountably irritating. "Alice didn't give me his name though. She said it was a secret. She had numerous admirers –"

"Who?"

"Umm. Rob."

"Rob what?"

"I don't know; I may not even have the Christian name right. He's a groom here –"

"Groom." He dashed off another note. "And?"

"John? Jim? His father keeps a tavern in Leatherhead. Bill . . ."

"Bill what?"

"I couldn't say. I wasn't Alice's chaperone, Mr. Stevens."

"No." He glowered at the notebook. "Anyone else?"

Anyone else? Alice had been marvelously indiscriminate, and there were lots of men about. Hines and his sons, Sean . . . Sean. Tiny hackles at the base of my scalp.

"No," I murmured, "no one."

"Thank you, Miss Hamilton. You'll be called at the inquest, probably Friday. I should appreciate it if you didn't leave the county in the interim . . ."

I went up the stairs, my feet seeming not to touch the gleaming marble, my temples throbbing. Sean? I removed my dress – my fingernails caught on the buttons – and sank onto the bed. Sean?

Mary had confided to Alice that something "very odd" was happening at Ashwood. Had Alice, curious Alice, wheedled the particulars? Had Alice, shrewd Alice, unraveled the plot? Had Alice, greedy Alice, glimpsed a literally golden opportunity?

She would have approached Sean obliquely,

198

no doubt, perhaps suggesting "a chat" after dinner. But housemaids do not make overtures – romantic or otherwise – to the master of the house, and Sean would have seen through her at once. Would have exploited her notorious weakness by proposing a rendezvous of a considerably more intimate nature. Would have sworn her leeringly to silence. Would have dallied with her till everyone was safely asleep, hitched a trap, driven her to that secluded embankment. Would have disguised her execution by making it appear the work of a blood-crazed lunatic. . . .

No! No! No! I inwardly shrieked. It was impossible, impossible. . . . But no more impossible than that Alice's death was a coincidence, unrelated to the previous violence at Ashwood.

I closed my eyes and saw her – carved up like a Christmas goose – and staggered to the water basin and was thoroughly sick.

There were two visitors from London the next day. The first – a gaunt, stooped, balding man – was pacing the entry hall when I went down for breakfast. I had forgone dinner and was indecently ravenous, and only after I had served myself from the sideboard did I ask his identity.

"Inspector Colby," Glynis said.

"Coleman," Sean corrected.

"Coleman. He's from Scotland Yard."

"And he's come down to investigate Alice's death?"

"Well, I doubt it's a social call." Glynis peevishly attacked her eggs.

"Why?" I wondered aloud.

"I'm sure I couldn't guess. It's exceedingly tiresome. Here we are, virtual prisoners in our own home, and all because Alice behaved like a common prostitute."

Caitlin blushed but continued to eat. How peculiar. Alice's grisly murder had not distressed her half so much as the innocuous gig accident. Sean, on the other hand, was pushing his food around his plate, tasting nothing. . . .

Inspector Coleman accosted me as I left the dining room and requested a private word. He ushered me into the library, where I perched in a chair. He began by restating Inspector Stevens's questions, and I framed my responses with care.

I had not consciously evaluated my position, but I had – while lying awake through most of the night – realized that I could not implicate Sean in Alice's murder. I had no proof, and if he were to be arrested on the strength of my hysterical accusations. . . . So I spoke again of Rob and Jim-John and Bill, and the inspector, I inferred, had heard it all before; at any rate, he took no notes. He inaugurated his new line of inquiry very casually.

"You recently came down from London, Miss Hamilton?"

"Yes. Not quite two weeks ago."

"And have you run across any acquaintances here?"

"Hardly. I'm afraid you've been misinformed, Mr. Coleman." I elucidated my background, my brief stay in the city. "So, you see, I'm a stranger in England myself."

"Umm. Perhaps you've met someone from London though?"

"Not so far as I remember." My heart bounded with hope. "Why? Do you have a suspect?"

"I could scarcely say that. However, we have had a rash of maniacal killings in recent years. Jack the Ripper, the Shoreditch Slasher. But then those were fully reported in the press, and one tends to feel this might be an imitation –"

Yes, I agreed despondently, one does. He waved me out, and I plodded up to Mercy's room. Alice had "passed away," I told her gently. She exploded into tears, and I distracted her with a long, largely fictional biography of Sacajawea. It was almost lunchtime when I finished and trudged back down the stairs, where I encountered the second visitor gazing myopically at the grandfather clock.

"Giles!" I was so happy to see him that the familiarity slipped out, and I bit my lip.

"No, it's quite all right. Indeed I should be flattered – Linnet, may I say? How perfectly ghastly about Miss Milton. I came down as soon as I heard; it was in all the morning papers –"

I led him to the drawing room, and he chattered on. He had located a copy of Edward's will, he said, and had found it unremarkable. He had no news of Robin. He wouldn't have journeyed down at all except he'd read of Alice's "gruesome" demise, and "as your solicitor, I thought to accompany you to the inquest –" A grand lie, exposed when he asked, with elaborate indifference, "And how is Miss Ashworth bearing up?"

"I shall let you judge for yourself. Luncheon should be ready, and I insist you stay."

Sean was "occupied," Glynis announced regretfully. "If we'd known you were coming, Mr. Chapman –"

But her syrupy charms were lost on Giles, who had eyes only for Caitlin. He planned to

202

attend the inquest, he revealed, but had yet to secure a hotel room.

"You must lodge here then," Caitlin purred.

"Oh, I couldn't, Miss Ashworth. I shouldn't wish to inconvenience you –"

"Inconvenience? Don't be silly. We've plenty of room, and Mrs. Abbott always cooks for an army . . ."

They parried back and forth, but Giles's heart wasn't in it, and Caitlin won handily. Immediately upon the conclusion of the meal, they excused themselves to attend his luggage and "look round the gardens a bit." Glynis sniffed.

"What a very tiresome fellow. But a splendid match for poor, dear Caitlin, I suppose."

So it seemed; by teatime Mrs. Abbott was humming under her breath and predicting a wedding within the year.

"They'll have to wait some months, of course, what with Miss Ashworth's brothers being so recently deceased. They'll be champing at the bit, I'll wager. Ed Abbott and I were engaged for just six weeks, and the time hung heavy on our hands, I can tell you. But it was well worth it; we were happily married for almost thirty years –"
She dabbed at her eyes with one corner of

her apron. "It strikes me as appropriate, Miss Hamilton."

"What does?"

"That Alice should have brought them together, so to speak. She was high on romance, Alice was."

"Did you talk to Inspector Coleman?" I asked.

"Yes. As did everyone else. He's barking up the wrong tree, miss. Jack the Ripper indeed! I set him straight, I did, told him about those fiendish gypsies. . . ."

I went to the dining room half an hour before dinner, hoping to find Giles alone. A place had been laid and a chair drawn up next to Caitlin's, and he was sitting in the chair, toying with the silverware, staring besottedly into space. I cleared my throat.

"Linnet."

His disappointment was unmistakable, and I managed an inward grin. "Sorry," I said dryly. "I wanted to talk to you."

"Are you nervous about the inquest then? It's a simple procedure, but we can review it if you like –"

"No, this has nothing to do with the inquest; it predates Alice's death. Actually, I was headed up to London yesterday when – when – The fact is, Giles, I'm most displeased with the administration of Ashwood." As I had with Inspector Coleman, I exercised extreme caution, never implying that the gig's errant wheel and the ruptured bridge were anything but accidents. I'm wondering what sort of legal recourse we have. Mr. Carlisle himself once remarked that he could be judged unfit –"

"Not on the basis of two random incidents." Giles shook his head. "Now if there's some indication that he's embezzling funds, plunging the estate into debt –" He raised his eyebrows interrogatively, and I answered him with silence. "Well, there you are then. Though I shall be happy to speak to him –"

"No! No, that won't be necessary."

Caitlin came in then – radiant, almost pretty – and Giles leaped out of his chair and rushed forward to meet her.

We all attended the inquest – all except Mercy and Lady Margaret – which, unfortunately, lent it the air of a holiday outing. Alf was called up first and, patiently prodded by the coroner, stammered out his story. He was "just walking about," as he often did in the mornings, when he spotted "something" in the ditch along the road. He moved closer and realized it was Alice's body.

"And what did you do then, Mr. Hines?"

205

"Nothing right then. I went back up to the stables. . . ."

He was dismissed.

The doctor who had performed the postmortem took the stand next. His testimony was long and altogether too graphic, and I was feeling distinctly queasy when he stepped down.

Then: "Miss Linnet Hamilton."

The questions had grown drearily familiar by now. Yes, I was Linnet Hamilton, Mrs. Justin Ashworth's sister and the governess at Ashwood. Yes, I had reached the stable last Wednesday morning to find Alf in a state of "excitement." Yes, he had directed me to a ditch beside the road, where he had pointed out Miss Alice Milton's corpse. Yes, I had seen Alice alive about six the previous evening.

"And at that time she told you of an engagement?"

"That's correct."

"An engagement with a gentleman?"

"Yes."

"She clearly stated that she intended to meet a man?"

I felt my brow furrow. Had she? "No, she said she had an engagement; that was all."

"Then why did you assume it was with a man, Miss Hamilton?"

"Well, Alice – Alice –" There was a titter from the back of the room. "I just did."

Inspector Stevens droned his piece, and Mrs. Abbott was called. She knew "nothing about the girl," she admitted. "She claimed to be from Hampshire –"

"But had no references?"

"Well, she was very young, and we were in desperate need of a maid . . ."

There were no further witnesses. The jury deliberated under five minutes before returning its verdict: "willful murder by some person unknown."

Giles apparently persuaded himself that he was duty-bound to stay on for the funeral, and the following morning we trooped to St. Andrew's. The majestic, impersonal Anglican service reminded me of Father's funeral. Hard to believe he had been dead for less than two months; I had, I reflected wryly, made a magnificent muck of my life in that brief interval.

Alice was laid to rest in the churchyard – ". . . ashes to ashes, dust to dust . . ." – and then, as though a great book had snapped shut, we turned back to the world. Sean had surrendered his place in the landau to Giles and now set out for Ashwood on horseback. The rest of us drove to the station, where Giles was to take the next train to London.

It wasn't due for almost half an hour, and Giles and Caitlin strolled up and down the platform – heads close, hands, from time to time, clasping.

"Oh, for heaven's sake," Glynis grumbled. "One would think they could be more discreet, wouldn't one?"

I glanced at her out of the corner of my eye, sensing a bond between us. We envy them the simplicity of their love, don't we, Glynis? I asked her silently. We chose very poorly, you and I, when we chose Sean Carlisle . . .

The train came at last, and Giles boarded. Caitlin, lips quivering, resumed her seat in the carriage, and we ambled back to Ashwood, normalcy restored.

And what was that: normalcy? I had no immediate fears for Mercy's safety; whether or not Sean had engineered Alice's cruel death, I thought it unlikely he'd undertake another. Not with Inspectors Stevens and Coleman nosing about the premises. But how long could I count on their unwitting protection? Sooner or later, if they did not bring Alice's murderer to justice, they would give up. And then?

Giles had dashed my legal hopes to bits. So was I to remain at Ashwood for ten years, a dozen, ever in Sean's thrall, ever wary of him? What was my alternative? I hadn't, as

Mr. Parker would have said, two nickels to rub together. . . .

Alf reined the horses smoothly in and handed us out of the landau. Slow? Yes. But he was whistling a cheerful, off-key tune, and we were mired in depression. We separated wordlessly in the entry hall, and I trudged up the stairs.

Mercy had pestered me with questions about Alice's funeral, had, in fact, begged to attend, but I had refused. A mistake? I wondered now. The child could not be spared indefinitely; her brief existence had been all too fraught with tragedy. I was wretchedly unprepared to address the mysteries of death and the afterlife (if indeed there was one), but I heaved a deep sigh and lifted a hand to knock on her door. Sean's voice boomed into the corridor.

"You must remember more than that, Mercy."

A long, unintelligible response.

"Oh, come now; has no one ever told you you're not to lie? I should hate to have to spank you."

The merest suggestion of piping protest.

"Well, Aunt Linnet may have believed that, but I don't. You're much too clever to have forgotten. Now we shall review it all again —"

I stormed through the door, literally trembling with anger. Mercy was cowering in the chair, Sean looming over her. He was so tall; he must seem quite enormous to her, like one of Mary's giants. . . .

"I believe it's time for your nap," I said shrilly.

"I don't take naps, anymore, Aunt Linnet. I've just had lunch —"

"And today you shall have a nap. And Cousin Sean will wait for me in my room because I'm exceedingly anxious to talk to him —"

She fought me like a fish, repeatedly squirming out of my grasp, but eventually I stripped off her dress and shoved her into bed. I had exhausted my meager store of Indians, and I spun a convoluted tale of a princess-turned-squirrel; why I selected this particular transformation, I don't recall. Her breathing became deep, even, and I crept out of the room.

"How dare you?" Sean was lounging against my doorjamb, but I detected an underlying tension in his easy pose. "She's scarcely more than an infant; how dare you browbeat her —"

"I'm sorry it appeared that way," he said stiffly. "I required some information —"

"And I can well imagine what it was. Let

me assure you that Mercy suspects nothing. You needn't eliminate her on that account. In fact, I should assume myself the logical target now you've rid yourself of Alice –"

"Alice!" He bolted upright, his eyes wide with shock. "You think I killed Alice?"

"Oh, I don't know what to think." The accumulated pressures and disappointments of the preceding few days swelled in my throat, prickled behind my eyelids. "You'll contend it was a hideous coincidence –"

"Linnet, listen to me –"

"No, you listen to me." He had again seared my jumbled thoughts into order. "You've won, Sean; I can't fight you any longer. I shall go up to London on Monday and try to make an arrangement with my aunt. Barring that, I shall seek another position. I shall leave Mercy here, and I'm sure you won't be so foolish as to harm her. I've mentioned the 'accidents' to Mr. Chapman, and I shall certainly discuss them with Aunt Jane and Uncle Henry as well. And I'm giving you fourteen years, am I not? You'll have reduced Ashwood to nothing by then, I expect, but I shan't ask any embarrassing questions. I'm offering you a 'deal,' as my American friends would put it. Let Mercy live for another week, another two, and you can have this bloody place. You and Glynis and Lady Margaret can pick its bones at your leisure. I shan't interfere, not ever; you can all go to the devil as far as I'm concerned."

"Linnet –"

I slammed the door, sagged against it, thought I heard him say something. "Be careful"? No, he wouldn't have said that. I ran across the room and threw myself on the bed, my vulgar bravado disintegrating in a rush. I had kept my emotions in check for two months and five thousand miles, and now they bubbled up, and I sobbed and sobbed till I had rendered myself absolutely empty.

ELEVEN

The next day was Sunday, but we did not go to church; there was, I believe, tacit agreement that we had seen enough of the Almighty during the week just past. It was a dreary day – gray, humid, punctuated with frequent thunderstorms – and Mercy was restless and fretful. We poked around the nursery and purloined several ancient articles of dress. These Mercy modeled for me, becoming, in turn, Queen Victoria, the Duke of Wellington, and "Sacajula." She soon tired of her sport, however, and sank into her chair, fairly swallowed up by the great hoopskirt.

"I want to go somewhere," she whined.

I had prayed for just such an opening. "And so do I," I said brightly. "I'm going up to London tomorrow, Mercy. I'll be away for a few days, but when I return we shall leave Ashwood."

"London? Has Mama come back then?"

I started guiltily; I had nearly forgotten Robin. "No, she hasn't. But we – you and I – shall find a wonderful place to live –"

"In London?" she persisted.

"Not necessarily. But there are lots of lovely spots, dear."

"Paris then," she said with finality.

I sighed, wishing I had not so impulsively burned my bridges. I entertained scant hope of making "an arrangement" with Aunt Jane, and the way to a new post was strewn with obstacles. I was a woman alone, devoid of experience, burdened with a child. . . . I quelled a rising wave of panic.

"Not Paris," I said, mindful of my primitive French. "Scotland perhaps. It's a beautiful country, they say. Or Ireland. Your grandmother was Irish, you know."

I displayed Mother's miniature and endowed her with a splendid heritage:

descent from royalty, a vague relationship to St. Patrick – well, as Sean had pointed out, all the Irish were cousins. . . . Sean. Must I forever think of Sean?

Shortly after five Mercy's dinner was brought up by Alice's replacement – a plump, sullen girl named May. I reminded her I would require a bath at seven sharp, and she responded with a martyred grimace. I stalked to my room, thankful that May's and my association would be a brief one.

Glynis had learned of my imminent departure and was positively aglow with good will.

"What a sad occasion," she cooed, as soon as we had sat down. "But then we mustn't be selfish. May I propose a toast?" She lifted her wineglass. "To Linnet: a safe journey and much success."

"You're leaving, Linnet?"

Caitlin's relief was unmistakable, and my eyes flickered from her to Sean. Why didn't you tell me, Caitlin? I asked her silently. I never would have loved him . . . But I would have. I did. Nothing could have changed that, and nothing ever would.

"Yes," I said.

"You have a position?"

"Not yet."

"But Linnet will have no trouble," Glynis

gushed. "She's so very clever, and the world is so very small these days –" She had apparently consigned me to a pest-ridden outpost in remotest Africa.

"I should like to get an early start," I said to Sean. "If Alf could have a trap ready about nine –"

"Alf has been instructed," Sean interrupted coldly.

Instructed in mischief? Surely not; another faulty wheel would be altogether too obvious.... I sensed Sean's eyes upon me, lowered my own, and gulped noisily at my soup.

In my room the lamp had been lit and the bed haphazardly turned down. I changed into my dressing gown, laid out the clothes I would wear to London, packed the rest. I missed Alice dreadfully. She had driven me half mad with her incessant chatter and her inconvenient "engagements," but now that she was gone . . . I thrust her freckled specter away and crawled into bed.

But Alice had never been easily snubbed, and she continued to haunt me. It had been so when Father died, I recalled: days of frantic, heedless activity followed by delayed shock, emptiness. And his death had been – I groped for the right word – acceptable: an aging man's graceful surrender to the ravages of time. Whereas Alice. . . .

"It's not like the other one."

I had quite forgotten Alf's remark, and I frowned into the darkness. An idle comment? I wondered. I thought not; he had said it twice. No, three times. "It's not like the other one." What other one? The unfortunate girl who had fallen prey to Mrs. Abbott's gypsies? Alf would have been a mere toddler at the time, unlikely to hear of the event, much less remember it. And it *had* been like Alice's death. If, against all odds, Alf did remember, why had he dredged up the differences rather than the appalling similarities?

I doubted it was important, but I made a drowsy mental note to ask him about it.

May was an hour late and – as if that were not sufficiently heinous – sloshed half my bath on the Turkish rug. I leaped into the tub, found its dregs distinctly tepid, and dressed with gnashing teeth. It was five to nine when I swooped through the dining room, grabbed a scone, and marched to the stable, scattering cold crumbs in my furious wake.

The trap, miraculously, was ready. Alf was absently stroking the mare, and I, feeling exceedingly foolish, stooped and examined each of the brougham's four wheels. When I straightened, Alf was staring at me, his brow deeply furrowed.

"Well, it never hurts to check," I laughed nervously. "We shouldn't want to lose a wheel, should we?" He did not respond, but I sensed, almost smelled, an instinctive, animal caution. "As the gig lost a wheel," I said slowly. "You remember that, don't you? Did you hitch the trap that day, Alf?"

"Yes'm."

"Did someone suggest that you – play with the wheel?"

"No."

"Then perhaps someone helped you." His eyes flickered, went blank. "Was that it, Alf? Was someone else at the coach house? Mr. Carlisle maybe?"

"No'm."

"No? Mr. Carlisle wasn't there?"

"No'm."

I would have wagered my last dollar that he was lying, but it was past, and I had neither the time nor the will to pursue it. "I was wondering about another thing, Alf. When we found Alice's – when we found Alice, you said it wasn't like the other one. What other one was that?"

"I dunno," he mumbled.

"Well, you do, of course; otherwise you wouldn't have said it. Now let's think about it, Alf. Was it something that happened when

217

you were a little boy?"

"No." A quick, firm shake of the head.

"It was much more recent then."

"I dunno."

"*Think* about it! It isn't every day one stumbles on a corpse –" But I had left him far behind. "Very well, we shall start at the beginning. Alice was just off the road. Was the other one near the road as well?"

"I dunno."

He probably didn't, I conceded. He probably recalled – if sporadically – a wounded deer, a butchered beef. . . .

"Very well," I said again. "My luggage is upstairs, Alf."

He didn't move. His eyes had never left me, and I became uncomfortably aware of their direction. He was gazing, not at my face but frankly, squarely at my bosom. It was easy to forget that Alf was a man. . . . I stepped back, but he was faster than I. His arm snaked out and caught me off balance, and I fell against him.

"Pretty," he said.

For one awful moment I thought he was speaking – in his singsong voice – of me. I eased away, not wishing to excite him, and felt myself drawn up. I glanced down and saw that he was fondling my cameo locket. I wore it always but usually inside my dress; evidently it had slipped out while I was looking at the wheels.

"It is pretty, isn't it?" I said shakily. "It's very old; it belonged to my grandmother."

He dropped it as abruptly as he had seized it, turned on his heel, and strode into the stable. I gaped after him, my vision blurring with rage. He was simple, yes, but this was too much, this brazen abandonment in a muddy coach yard. . . . He bounded back to my side, grinning triumphantly, his fist clenched.

"See, miss? I got one, too."

He spread his hand to reveal a locket identical to mine. I took it, snapped it open, and met Mother's placid, violet eyes.

"Where did you find this, Alf?" I asked.

"In the carriage." He nodded toward the brougham. "I should have give it back, I reckon."

"Well, how could you?" I said soothingly. "I'm sure you didn't discover it till Robin had boarded the train –"

He wasn't listening. "I thought on it, but Miss Ashworth didn't say nothing about it, so I kept it."

"Miss Ashworth? Caitlin?"

"Yes'm."

"What does Miss Ashworth have to do with the locket?"

"Well, it's hers, miss."

"But it isn't. It's my –" I stopped. "Why did you think it was Caitlin's, Alf?"

"She had it on." He traced a vague ellipse on the front of his shirt. "And after she got out of the trap –"

Intuition struck like lightning, and I saw it all. They were the same size, nearly of an age, and in the dim light of dawn. . . . It had been Caitlin in the carriage, Caitlin masquerading as Robin, and Robin. . . . Dear God, I sprinted away, leaving Alf to chant his explanation behind me, and raced across the lawn, clutching the locket in one soggy palm.

I had not been to Caitlin's room, but Sean had identified it during our tour of the house. I dashed through the music room – dodging the harp and a sagging music stand – and into the wing beyond. Caitlin's was the first door on the left, and I burst in without knocking.

It looked like Mercy's room – neat, frilly, blue. Odd that I should remember. Caitlin was seated at a miniature desk, busily writing. A letter to Giles? She started and laid her pen aside.

"Linnet! Have you come to say good-bye then? I'd hoped to see you again –"

"No, I've come to return something." Some childish sense of drama impelled me to dangle the locket an inch before her nose. "Do you recognize it, Caitlin?"

She paled. "Oh, dear."

"Indeed." I shoved the locket in my pocket. *"Where is my sister?"*

"I don't know," she whimpered.

"For God's sake, Caitlin!" My language had deteriorated most shockingly. "You dressed in her clothes and made a great show of departing for the station. Which means Robin didn't. Robin is here, here at Ashwood. Now where?"

"I don't know! I swear it, Linnet; I don't know!" She stood up and began pacing the floor, tripping over her skirt, wringing her hands. "Mother told me to do it —"

"Mother?" I echoed sharply. It didn't fit. "Lady Margaret instructed you to impersonate Robin? Why?"

"I don't know!" Half sobbing now. "It was for the good of the family, she said, and I was to ask no questions. Hines came after me very early in the morning, about four, I think. Mother had Robin's things in her room — a dress and a bonnet and the locket, of course, and the rest packed in Robin's portmanteau. She told me to put on Robin's clothes and sent Hines back for a dress and bonnet of mine. Those he put in the portmanteau as well. Then Mother told me to meet Alf in the coach yard. The brougham was hitched, and

221

I got in, and Alf loaded the portmanteau. We went down to the road, and the gig was there, Colin Hines at the reins –"

"Colin?"

"Yes. Hines met us a few minutes later; apparently he'd cut through the woods. We drove about halfway to Long Hill Farm and stopped beside a grove of beeches. Hines told me to change into my own clothes, and I went into the trees – it was horrible, Linnet, degrading – Hines took Robin's clothes and put them in the portmanteau. Then Hines and I got in the gig, and he drove me back. Not all the way; there's a rear drive that ends about half a mile from the house, and we left the gig there and walked through the garden. Hines escorted me to my room –"

"And later in the morning he brought back the gig, as though returning from an errand. And Alf came back in the brougham, as though he'd delivered Robin to the station."

"Yes."

"And Robin's things?"

"I'm not sure. Colin was digging in the grove when I left."

"They were buried then."

"I presume so."

They and Robin, too; I knew it as surely as if I had witnessed that dawn-gray scene in the woods. "Did it not occur to you to wonder

222

what had happened to her?" My voice was shrill with grief and frustration.

"I've wondered nothing else, Linnet! I was terrified for you; that's why I begged you to leave —"

"Oh, Caitlin." My mind was in shreds. They had killed Robin — Lady Margaret and Hines and his sons — and it made no sense, none at all. "Is there anything else?" I asked dully.

"No."

She was a very bad liar; her eyes strayed to the wardrobe. I stepped toward it, but she was amazingly agile; she reached it before I did and plastered herself against it.

"Please, Linnet." The tears were streaming down her tiny, pinched face. "Please don't. Just go; go while you can —"

"Get out of my way, Caitlin." I yanked her aside and peered behind the wardrobe. And glimpsed a frame, a heavy carved picture frame. . . .

"It was you in the nursery." I wasn't especially surprised; the world had turned upside down. "Why?"

"I didn't want you to see it."

"Why not?"

"Mother told me to hide it. She couldn't bear to destroy it, she said, but I was to secure it where no one would ever find it —"

"It's Justin, isn't it?"

"Yes. Linnet!"

She clawed at my arm, but I was stronger than she. I pulled the painting out and held it in front of me. It had been executed on a grand scale – with the picture gallery in mind – and my perspective was poor. I thrust it out as far as I could and cocked my head.

A handsome man. Black hair, black eyes: Mercy's father. Dark complexion: Sean's cousin. A handsome man, but that was all.

I set it on the floor, moved back, and felt a vague stir of recognition. Different, something different – I sketched in sideburns, a mustache, a black beard, and Justin disappeared.

I was looking at a competent if rather uninspired portrait of Rodman Thatcher.

TWELVE

I stared at the picture, eerily calm. Of course. I chided myself at my obtuseness. Of course, Justin was alive, and that explained everything.

The stable boy – what was his name? – Garrett had been sacrificed first. The unfortunate fellow had been about Justin's size, no doubt, and – literally cremated, outfitted with Justin's accessories – had readily passed the postmortem. Which had left Lady Margaret with the distinctly awkward presence of a "dead" son.

But she, with Hines's devoted assistance, had risen to the occasion. The tenant was summarily ejected from Long Hill Farm, and Colin Hines brought down in his place. Colin was the perfect warden: loyal, tough, clever, "touchy," he could be counted upon to play his part to a faultless hilt. But it wasn't enough.

The servants were a problem. One could never know when a maid or groom might seize an idle moment to wander over to Long Hill Farm. Might recognize the late Dr. Ashworth – hirsute disguise notwithstanding – in his new role. Better safe than sorry; the staff were dismissed. All except Hines and Alf and, purely by chance, Betsy, whose faulty eyesight rendered her wonderfully innocuous. As an added precaution, Justin's portrait was hidden away, lest any of the new servants note the similarity between Rodman Thatcher and Justin Ashworth. And the new servants were carefully screened, no one taken on who had any prior connection with Ashwood.

Enter Robin. To ask for money? I couldn't

be sure, and I let it go. She had, at any rate, insisted on a tour of Ashwood. Had spotted Rodman/Justin at Long Hill Farm. Had . . .

But I couldn't bear to think about it, and I rushed on. With Robin eliminated, Justin was again secure, and Lady Margaret heaved a sigh of relief. Short-lived. She had scarcely disposed of Robin when Robin's sister reared her ugly head. With – to make matters infinitely worse – Justin's daughter in tow.

I had indeed caught her unawares, I reflected. She had expected to order me off – like the servants, like the tenants – and my stubborn Irish refusal had disarmed her. Had she made her offer that very first night, before I could talk to Mrs. Abbott . . . But she hadn't.

Old, ill, emotionally exhausted, she had needed time to assess her options, and she had set me free.

Though not to explore at will. I hadn't met Justin – she was immensely comforted to learn that – but there might be a miniature, a photograph. . . . She instructed Hines to keep me away from Long Hill Farm, and Hines relayed the message to Alf. But Alf allowed me to slip through his clumsy fingers, for which carelessness he received a thorough dressing down. And Colin – no wonder Colin was short; he was horrified to find me, of all people, dallying with his precious charge. The sticky encounter ended happily, however; it was clear I had not recognized Justin.

Mercy was another case entirely; it was too much to hope she wouldn't know her father if ever she saw him. Mary was appointed the child's jailer, cautioned not to let the girl out of her sight. But Mary got ill, Alice as well, and Linnet mucked up the works by proposing an excursion to Long Hill Farm. Sean directed Alf to hitch the gig, and Hines, in desperation, loosened the wheel. If the accident proved fatal, so be it; if not, Justin was safe for another day.

But they – Lady Margaret and Justin and the Hineses – could not continue to live from day to day, hour to hour. I'd decided to stay at Ashwood, and the situation was intolerable. Mercy must be permanently removed. Victoria was abducted, the bridge sawed through. . . .

Mercy escaped, but Alice died before the following dawn. Why? Had she, despite Lady Margaret's vigilance, somehow identified Justin? She must have, but why had she been killed in such bestial fashion? Why – back at the head of the maze – had she been killed at all? She or Garrett or Robin? What was Justin's secret that it demanded this terrible tribute of deceit and death?

"Linnet?"

Caitlin's voice jarred me from my dark reverie, and I realized, as I had on the shore of the lake, that mere seconds had elapsed.

"What is it, Linnet?"

"Justin is alive," I said levelly.

"I suspected as much." Her little face was white, empty.

"Dear God, Caitlin. Why?"

"Mother told me not to go to Long Hill Farm. Not ever again. It was just after I hid the picture –"

"That isn't what I meant. Why was it necessary? What has Justin done?"

"I don't know. I speculated it was malpractice. A lawsuit, criminal prosecution even –"

"And that justifies his abandonment of wife and child? That justifies three deaths?"

"Deaths?" She seemed, if possible, to shrink.

"The body in the stable, Caitlin. Whom did you suppose him to be?"

"I assumed it was an accident."

"A most convenient accident. And Robin's disappearance? You knew that wasn't an accident."

"But I never believed –" Great tears welled behind the heavy spectacles.

228

"That they'd killed her?" I said brutally. "Then what of Alice? Alice is indisputably dead."

"But she was murdered by gypsies."

"Oh, Caitlin." I tried to hate her, but she was – no less than I – a cat's-paw. "The brougham is hitched, and Alf is waiting for me. I shall go into town as though nothing had happened and bring back Inspector Stevens. In the meantime, you're to locate Sean. Explain the situation and ask him to meet us at Long Hill Farm. Give me a five-minute advantage –"

I sauntered through the music room and out the front door, strolled across the lawn. Hines, if he was about, must not guess anything to be amiss. I flashed Alf a pleasant smile.

"Well, that's taken care of," I said, as though my frenzied flight had been altogether routine. "We shall have to hurry though, so I shall let myself in –"

I watched Alf mount the box, then opened the door of the carriage. From the far side of the seat, Hines gave me a cool nod.

"I trust you don't mind, Miss Hamilton? I have an errand in town."

I groped for the proper, normal response. "As long as I'm not held up," I said haughtily. "I'm late as it is."

I took my seat and closed the door, and

the brougham lurched to a start. Hines and I had never pretended to friendship; he would expect no conversation. I stared straight ahead as we trotted down the drive. We reached the road and turned left, in the direction of Long Hill Farm.

"Need I remind you I'm in a hurry, Hines?" I snapped. "We haven't time to stop at Long Hill Farm. I've a train to catch –"

"Do you indeed, Miss Hamilton?"

His face was impassive, but there was an undertone of insolence in his voice, and I felt a laggard twinge of alarm.

"I certainly do, and Mr. Carlisle will be most annoyed –"

"Haven't you forgotten something?"

"Not that I'm aware of."

"Your luggage? I was given to understand you'd be away a week or more, and you've never struck me as the absentminded sort. But perhaps your plans have changed."

My heart bounded into my throat. He knew; he knew; he was driving me to Long Hill Farm like an animal to slaughter. . . . My hand crept toward the door handle, and he grasped my opposite elbow.

"You're a clever young woman," he said admiringly. "Very – levelheaded, may I say? Not a family trait, I gather. Your sister acted very unwisely."

My eyes roamed the interior of the trap, darted through the windows. Escape was out of the question: there were two of them, and the road was deserted. But Sean was coming; time was my ally. . . .

"Unwisely? In what way?"

"She exposed her hand. Shocking in view of her background." He smiled mirthlessly. "Your father was a gambler, I'm told."

Who lost; who always lost. . . . "What *was* her hand, Hines? The will? That could hardly have been a secret."

"Actually, Lady Margaret had hoped it was. Mr. Justin has never had the slightest interest in Ashwood, and he didn't remember whether he had mentioned the will to your sister or not. Apparently, he had."

"And Robin came to Ashwood to claim Mercy's inheritance."

"Yes."

"And declined Lady Margaret's generous offer of settlement."

"There was no offer. A grave error on Lady Margaret's part." He sighed. "But the poor woman had no ready cash –"

"Oh, come now, Hines. She unearthed twenty thousand pounds in a matter of days."

"But days made all the difference, Miss Hamilton. It was clear you didn't know about the will, not at the beginning, and

231

Lady Margaret had time to make suitable arrangements. She entrusted me with her personal jewelry, which I took up to London. It was appraised at thirty thousand pounds."

I had had ample room to bargain, I reflected wryly.

"In your sister's case, Lady Margaret had no such leeway, and she was forced to improvise. The estate was deeply in debt, she said, and while Mrs. Ashworth was welcome to it, it would be nothing but a millstone round her neck. Mr. Justin had left Mrs. Ashworth a modest annuity, and Lady Margaret suggested she be content with that."

"But Robin didn't believe her."

"No. She went to Mr. Carlisle and demanded a tour of the estate."

"During the course of which she saw Justin."

"Yes. He's been exceedingly rash, a constant thorn in Colin's flesh –" Hines pursed his lips. "Be that as it may, Mrs. Ashworth lost her head. Had she returned quietly to London – but she didn't. She confronted Lady Margaret. She knew Justin was alive, she said. Furthermore, she knew why we were hiding him; her journal – she waved it in Lady Margaret's face – contained the particulars. She'd observed that Ashwood was thriving, but she didn't want the place,

232

didn't, in fact, want anything further to do with the Ashworths. If Lady Margaret would give her twenty thousand pounds, she would surrender the journal and never darken our door again."

Two wrongs, soon to become three. "So Robin set the price on Ashwood," I mused. "And the journal? What was in the journal?"

"Lady Margaret couldn't agree, of course." Hines ignored my question. "Even without the journal, Mrs. Ashworth could have gone to the police at any time. Lady Margaret begged an opportunity to consider the proposal —"

"And you killed Robin."

"Yes. I wish to assure you it was painless. And highly distasteful. And now —" His gray eyes clouded. "I'm truly sorry you had to become involved, Miss Hamilton. But when Alf informed me of your odd reaction to the locket . . ."

Clop-clop, clop-clop; the mare cantered along. We were nearing the beech grove, the spot where Robin was buried. Almost halfway there, and Hines's grip on my arm had never slackened.

"Alf *is* terribly loose-lipped," I said. "You really must do something about him. He remembers Robin's murder —"

"He can't possibly. He helped dig the

grave, but he didn't see the corpse. It – she was in the gig with Colin."

"He remembers nevertheless. He mentioned it when we found Alice's body. He calls Robin 'the other one.' "

Hines frowned. "He must have been referring to Mary."

"Mary!" Dear God, how many more?

"A most distressing episode." His voice fairly dripped regret. "Unfortunately, we needed her cooperation."

"She arranged Victoria's theft, I presume."

"Victoria?"

"The doll."

"Yes."

"Then you stole her."

"Yes."

"And took her to the island?"

"No, Alf was responsible for that. He dismantled the bridge on his way back and later swam out and retrieved the doll. He thought it was a game, but Mary was bound to draw dangerous conclusions. So I instructed her to leave Miss Mercy on the shore and report to Lady Margaret. In the interim I packed her things –"

"Waited for her in Lady Margaret's room and killed her. Late that night you hitched a trap and carted her off, her and everything she owned. Alf assisted again –"

234

"It was an extemporaneous project, Miss Hamilton. Colin had left for London before I could reach him. Alf will forget it in due course."

As he would forget me.... "And Alice? Was that your doing or Colin's?"

He looked at me quizzically. "You were not aware of your sister's suspicions then? I had wondered."

"Robin's suspicions? Robin was dead long before Alice."

"Yes. But Alice was not the first of Mr. Justin's victims."

"Justin!" The last piece crashed into place. "Oh, my God."

"He's very ill, I'm afraid." Hines emitted another sigh. "A sickness of the mind. The first incident occurred some twenty years ago: a dairymaid of dubious morals –"

"Who everyone assumed was killed by gypsies."

"Yes. I didn't sleep very well in those days, Miss Hamilton. I had lost my wife a few years since, and I was saddled with two young sons. Colin was precocious but frankly wild, and Alf – At any rate, I often rose in the middle of the night and wandered about the grounds. And that particular night I encountered Mr. Justin in the stable, his clothes soaked with blood. He made some excuse – I no longer

235

recall it – and I returned to bed. But the next morning when I learned of the murder, I went directly to Sir Robert."

"And blackmailed him."

"I don't like to think of it in those terms. I prefer to believe we had similar interests – Sir Robert and I. Each of us had a son. His stood to be hanged, and mine to become a ruffian. And each of us had the means to deliver the other's child. Blackmail? No, a business transaction."

"Your silence for Colin's education."

"Precisely."

"Was it a fair transaction, Hines? You unleashed a homicidal maniac –"

"You accuse me from hindsight, Miss Hamilton. Mr. Justin was only thirteen. The girl – Nan? Nell? – was a notorious tease, and I attributed Mr. Justin's action to a fit of adolescent frustration. Extreme, yes, but there was no reason to assume it would happen again. Nor did it. Not for better than eighteen years."

"And then?"

"And then there was another – incident."

"And Robin knew? Robin calmly recorded it in her journal?"

"Mrs. Ashworth recorded a number of seemingly disjointed events. Which, properly assembled, afforded a most damaging picture.

236

A pity I can't let you read the journal for yourself, but it had to be destroyed."

"Did Justin see it?" He shook his head. "Then what prompted your deadly little charade?"

"The London police interrogated Mr. Justin late last winter. They were not yet prepared to make an arrest, but he was clearly under sharp suspicion. He came down to Ashwood and confessed his plight to Lady Margaret, and she summoned me. Mr. Justin was in serious trouble, she told me, and I must help her save him. I was as much an accessory as she, and if he were arrested, the truth would come out. . . . We conferred for hours – the three of us – and eventually determined that Mr. Justin should appear to die."

So Garrett had been burned alive in the stable, Robin buried in a lonely beech grove, Mary. . . . What did it matter? I was next. We had turned into the drive of Long Hill Farm, and still he held me.

"Why did you choose to hide him here?" I nodded out the window. "It's much too close to Ashwood."

"We didn't. We intended him to go to Australia; in fact, I booked his passage. He was to stay at Long Hill Farm for two months, grow in his beard, gain or lose a stone. Then Mr. Edward died, and Lady

237

Margaret couldn't bear to let Mr. Justin leave. She wanted him nearby so he could visit from time to time, late at night –"

Mary's duke, Mercy's spectral duke. One question now, just one. "Whom did he kill, Hines? In London. What was the 'damaging picture' in Robin's journal?"

"The names would mean nothing to you, Miss Hamilton. But the press gave him a sobriquet that rather amused him." He flashed that humorless smile. "They called him the Shoreditch Slasher."

THIRTEEN

Why had it taken Robin so long to guess? She had written of Justin's violent behavior, his unpredictable hours, and surely she had observed his blood-spattered clothing. . . . But Mrs. McDonald had blamed the doctor's "ghastly operations," and no doubt Robin had as well. It wasn't till after Justin's "death" that, idly scanning her journal, she recognized the critical dates. She reviewed the newspapers, and her horrible suspicion was confirmed: the nights when Justin had come home so very late, so very bloody,

238

coincided with the grisly murders of the Shoreditch Slasher.

She could not – I recalled her last, desperate letter – "determine what to do." Conscience dictated a visit to the police, but what was the point? Justin was dead, or so she believed, and a posthumous scandal would serve only to blacken Mercy's name. Better, perhaps, that Justin's crimes be laid to rest with the man himself.

Edward died, and Robin could not suppress a selfish sigh of relief. Justin's "modest" annuity was utterly inadequate, and now Mercy had inherited a grand estate. Robin awaited a communication from the Ashworths' solicitors.

But a decent interval elapsed, and there was no communication. What was she to do? The Ashworths were wealthy, powerful; she, in severely straitened circumstances. A legal dispute might well be decided in Mercy's favor, but Robin couldn't afford to wage the battle. Her eyes strayed to the journal; did she not possess a "weapon"? Lady Margaret wouldn't wish to see Justin's name in shrieking headlines. Robin packed up the journal and traveled down to Ashwood, to her own fatal rendezvous with the Shoreditch Slasher.

The carriage eased to a halt, and Colin

Hines strode out of the house. Hines released me and clambered nimbly down from the trap, and I massaged my arm, which had grown quite numb. I reached for the door handle, then realized it was hopeless. There were three of them now – four. Justin sauntered out of the barn, and I could not help noticing a rusty stain on his trousers.

Time, I thought again; I needed time, but how much? I estimated we had left Ashwood some twenty minutes before. Five minutes later Caitlin had gone in search of Sean, and with any luck at all, she would have located him by now. Just – he would require another quarter of an hour to reach Long Hill Farm. And my captors were already deep in conversation, already spinning their lethal web. . . . I got out of the coach and walked across the yard, and they fell silent.

"Dr. Ashworth, I presume?" I looked directly into his black eyes, steeling myself for some shocking glimpse of evil, but there was none. He might have been a kindly, down-at-heels country physician.

"Must we be so formal?" There was a faint suggestion of brandy on his breath. "I should think, in view of our relationship –"

"I deplore our relationship. And I find it appalling that you should choose to mention it, with Robin buried not five miles away."

"A circumstance I deeply regret." He spoke with unmistakable sincerity, and I gazed at him, chilled, fascinated. "I was extremely fond of Robin. If only she hadn't seen me –"

"She wouldn't have if you'd stayed inside the barn," Colin snapped.

"I shan't be made a prisoner," Justin said airily.

"No, you've made that clear enough. And you see the bloody mess you've got us in."

"You're forgetting your place, Colin. And not for the first time. I shan't be ordered about –"

"Gentlemen, please!" Hines glared from one to the other. "We shall resolve our personal differences at another time. For the present –" He tossed his head at me.

Time. Time. I glanced casually toward the road, but it was damp; there would be no dust. . . . "And what of Mercy? Would you have regretted her death as well?"

"A painful topic, Miss Hamilton." Justin scowled at Hines. "The attempt on Mercy's life was made quite behind my back. Fortunately, Alice" – the name tripped smoothly off his tongue – "told me what had transpired, and I extracted Mother's promise that Mercy would not be harmed. Such a waste; such a tragedy. If I had been consulted at the start, Mary could have been

241

spared." A sigh of genuine remorse; dear God, what sort of two-headed monster was he?

"What will become of Mercy now?"

"I believe Aunt Jane can be persuaded to take her in. With you – gone" – he lowered his eyes – "and a handsome settlement from Mother – yes, Aunt Jane will perceive her Christian duty."

"And am I to 'disappear'?"

"That would be a trifle implausible, don't you agree? No, an accident will prove considerably more convincing."

"What – what kind of accident?"

"We shall discuss it in the trap," Hines interjected impatiently. "Saddle the horse, Colin, and follow when you can. You'll overtake us, I expect –"

Hines grabbed my arm and dragged me toward the brougham. I could bluff no longer; if Robin had exposed her hand, mine had been called.

"You're too late, Hines," I said. "Sean will be here at any moment."

"Sean!" He jerked me to a stop. "Carlisle? How can that be?"

"I sent Caitlin after him. She knows everything, Hines, *everything*, and she set out half an hour ago."

"Set out how?" Justin asked lazily.

"On her saddle horse, I presume –"

"But she doesn't have one, Miss Hamilton. She never has. Nor does she drive. Caitlin is terrified of horses; did she not tell you?"

I had given her no opportunity, I reflected dismally. I'd babbled my instructions and rushed out. . . .

"Apparently not. And if she's plodding the length and breadth of the estate in one of her dreadful skirts. . . . Nevertheless I shall chase her down." This to Hines: "I should hate Sean to get involved."

"But he will." My voice was shrill with burgeoning panic. "Caitlin knows, I tell you, and you can't just lock her away –"

"Can we not? Have you failed to observe how wonderfully obedient Caitlin is? Mother will arrange an extended holiday in Scotland – we have a summer home there – and in due time –" Justin shrugged.

Time. There it was again, and mine had run out. Caitlin would not have found Sean, not if she was afoot. And if she had; if, by some miracle, she had? Sean would ride to Long Hill Farm, expecting to meet Inspector Stevens, and there would be another "accident" . . .

Hines handed me correctly, primly, into the rig and climbed in after me. Alf, who had never left his perch, clucked to the mare, and we turned and trotted down the drive. From the window I saw Colin and Justin sprinting toward the barn.

"Am I to die in the trap?" I asked, perversely curious.

"Yes. There's a branch of the river not far ahead, overlooked by a bluff. A steep bluff, and the road is situated perilously near the brink. And the road – had you noticed? – is extremely slippery."

The coach, in unhappy confirmation, slithered to one side.

"And I shall go over – I and the mare and the rig."

"Yes."

"And Alf?"

"Alf will be found at the edge of the cliff, scratched and bruised but – praise be to God – alive."

"How do you propose to explain my presence beyond Long Hill Farm? I was going up to London –"

"But you changed your mind, didn't you; you left your luggage behind." He smiled blandly. "And who can explain a woman's whims, Miss Hamilton? Certainly not Alf. The poor fellow does well to carry out his instructions. Instructions that, in this instance, will prove fatal."

The rain had been heavier here. Alf had pulled up, but the carriage slid, recovered, slid again. There was a sound beside us, and I turned, my heart crashing against my ribs. But it was the gray horse, lathered, Colin astride. He reined in, and the gray slowed to our pace, the mud sucking at his hoofs.

We stopped. Colin dismounted, and Hines opened his window. "Get Alf down," he said. "I want you on the box." Colin asked a question I couldn't hear. "No, we shall tend to Alf after the rig goes over."

Colin stepped forward, and in a moment Alf clambered down, rather stiffly, and slogged through the mud, looking more befuddled than usual. Colin assumed his place on the box.

"Take her to two feet if you can," Hines directed through the window in front of us. "But stop if she gets skittish."

I felt the coach creep forward. Hines was a brave man, I admitted, my arm tensing beneath his fingers. I wouldn't have stayed in that trap for anything, not willingly, but he, except for a fine sheen of perspiration on his brow, seemed perfectly calm. There was a sickening lurch.

"What the devil?" Hines growled.

"She won't go any further, Pa. And she's four feet away, maybe five."

"You've got too damned civilized, Colin.

I'll do it myself. Get down and we'll exchange –"

"I'll have to back her up."

"You're not to back her up! You've plenty of room –"

Hines inched forward on the seat, inched toward the window, and, almost imperceptibly, his grip on my elbow relaxed. My other hand crept to the door, found the handle.

"Never mind; you can do it. Ease her a little to the right so she can't see the precipice." Another lurch; I willed myself not to stiffen. "Right, Colin! Hard right, then straight ahead; she'll think you're turning her away –"

The trap slid almost perpendicular to the mare, and Hines dropped my arm. It had happened so fast I'd lost my sense of direction. What lay beyond the door? The sheer drop to the river or the cool, safe mud? Did it matter? I'd improved my odds. I shoved the door open and – muttering a prayer to some outlandish composite of Zeus and Lady Luck and Father Stevens's Anglican God – threw myself out of the coach.

Noise; cacophony; the roar of death? I awaited the final thrust of pain – surely there was one – but I was absurdly comfortable. Cold, a bit slimy . . . The noise became an echo, and I lifted my head.

I was lying in the mud, encased to my neck in the mud, and the trap was gone. Alf was gazing over the bluff, and I struggled up and staggered to his side.

It was a long way down, a very long way. I could make out the rig and, I thought, the mare, but that was all. And God, whatever gods there are, forgive me: I was only sorry about the mare.

I groped instinctively for Alf's hand, and we stood there, refugees from a nightmare. Stood there for a minute, maybe two, and then I heard the drum of hoofbeats over my shoulder.

They were racing through the woods, short-cutting the road. Sean was in front, and he sat his mount well, as I would have expected. But Caitlin ... Dear God, Caitlin lacked a saddle, even a bridle, she was clinging to her horse's mane.

It was then, finally, that I burst into uncontrollable tears.

FOURTEEN

A year has passed since then, and sometimes it seems a score, a hundred. Sometimes it seems, indeed, that it never happened at all, that the muddy road and the bluff and the tangled trap in the river are images from an ancient, half-forgotten dream. And then there *is* a dream, and I live it all again, as though it had been yesterday. I hear Hines ("Right, Colin! Hard right . . ."), feel his iron fingers on my arm, feel the coach slipping beneath us, slithering toward oblivion. And I wake, not in that blessed bed of mud, but in an icy sweat, whimpering, and mumbling my garbled prayers. I reach for Sean, as I did then, and he holds me, as he did then, and I travel back, remember . . .

Sean leaping off his horse and sweeping me into his arms. Me clinging to him and sobbing my apologies and cloaking him with mud from shoulder to ankle. Him stepping back, smiling; me sensing that I had solved the last and most elusive puzzle. I have come Home, Father – I remember thinking that; I have truly come Home.

Then I went to Caitlin – I remember this

248

very clearly – and Caitlin was clutching her horse's ear – his ear! – and it should have been funny, but I could only cry. And Caitlin cried as well and leaned down to embrace me and nearly fell off the horse, and we laughed. And that – perhaps that was the beginning of the healing.

As for how long it took – the healing – I can't say. Maybe it isn't over; maybe it never will be.

We rode back to Ashwood, but I recall little of that. Only that Caitlin, having found her wings, stubbornly refused to relinquish her mount. So I sat pillion behind Sean. Alf took the gray, and Caitlin led our motley parade. Which was fitting, for her victory was greater, far greater, than mine.

Sean left me at the front door and went directly to Leatherhead to fetch Inspector Stevens. Mrs. Abbott – her ears fairly twitching – was waiting in the entry hall and trailed me up the stairs, panting forth an endless stream of questions. I wanted nothing in the world except a bath, and I gave her a rather sketchy account of the day's events. It was sufficient, however, to send her into transports of oohing and aahing, head-shaking and tongue-clicking.

"I knew it," she said triumphantly, when I had finished. "I didn't believe for an instant that Alice was done in by gypsies. And I'm not in the least surprised that Mr. Hines was in it up to his neck . . ."

Eventually, I prevailed on her to draw my bath, and by the time I had bathed and changed, the inspector had arrived.

His interrogation continued for hours, each of us being summoned to the drawing room in turn. When it was over, he placed Lady Margaret under house arrest, which I had expected, and Caitlin and Alf, which I had not.

"He can't!" I wailed to Sean.

We were seated in the library, and Sean touched a finger to his lips, reminding me that our jailer, a uniformed policeman, stood just in the hall.

"He can't," I hissed. "Alf isn't responsible for his actions, and Caitlin has always done precisely as she was told. Until today, and surely her conduct proves her innocence."

"The inspector can't make that determination, Linnet. If the coroner rules murder, they will have to appear before the magistrates."

"Then we must notify Giles."

"I already have; I telegraphed him immediately after I spoke with Stevens. Unless I badly miss my guess, he'll be down early in the morning."

He was calm, too calm. "This didn't come as a particular shock to you, did it?" I said.

"Yes and no. I'd no idea of Robin's death, or Mary's, but I'd suspected for some days that Justin was alive . . ."

It had started with the servants, he told me. He hadn't realized the staff was new till I mentioned it: "It struck me as odd. Then you commented on the removal of Justin's portrait from the gallery. I tossed out an explanation, but, in retrospect, it puzzled me."

Next was Lady Margaret's offer. "Where had she come by twenty thousand pounds? If it was Ashwood money, it wasn't Aunt Margaret's to spend. When I asked her about it, she convinced me the funds were hers, but what was her objective? The will specifically enjoined the heir to provide for Aunt Margaret; why was she so frantic to secure the estate for me?"

He was still mulling it over when I accused him of plotting Mercy's death. "It was all very provocative – the gig accident, the business with the doll, Mary's flight – but I was inclined to assume coincidence. Until I swam out to the island and found the doll had disappeared. Then I knew you were right."

"And you did nothing!"

"What would you have had me do? Someone was trying to kill Mercy, but who?

251

Why? As you'd so vehemently pointed out" – he flashed a wry grin – "I was the only one with a motive. I felt, as you did, that Mercy was temporarily safe, and I resolved to nose discreetly about. Had I not identified the culprit in a week, ten days, I intended to send you back to London."

"So you began your 'nosing about' –"

"I had no chance. Alice was killed that night, and I thought at once of Justin."

"Justin? Why Justin?"

"Mrs. Abbott was chattering about the murder that occurred in 1870, and I remembered it well because I was at Ashwood when it happened. Mother was ill – in fact, she died before Christmas – and Dad had sent me to Surrey for my summer holiday. Aunt Margaret was a social butterfly in those days, much too busy for me, and she turned me over to Justin. We were exactly the same age – thirteen that year – and everyone assumed we were bosom friends.

"But we weren't, not ever. There was something – something strange about Justin, and I generally tried to avoid him. At any rate, I'd been at Ashwood for, oh, three weeks, I suppose, and I was bored bloody stiff. And then there was this gruesome killing, practically within sight of the house, and I was enough of a child to think it terribly exciting.

"Justin, too. We raced to the scene as soon as we heard the news, but the police had already removed the corpse. We started poking around, and after about ten minutes I spotted a scrap of cloth peeping out from under a rock. I moved the rock away and uncovered a handkerchief fairly saturated with blood.

" 'Halloo, Justin!' I yelled. You can imagine how thrilled I was. 'Come see what I've found.'

"He walked over and stared at it, as though he'd turned to stone.

" 'Well, don't you see?' I said. 'It's the murderer's handkerchief.'

"He looked at it a while longer. 'It can't be,' he said at last. 'The police would have taken it.'

" 'The police didn't see it, silly. I expect he dropped it – the murderer, that is – and it blew away a bit, and later someone kicked the rock down on top of it. We must take it to town. We'll hitch the gig –'

" 'We shall do no such thing,' he said. 'We shall simply make fools of ourselves. There's a good deal of hunting hereabouts –'

" 'Well, the police know that, stupid. They won't jump to any hasty conclusions. But we have to take it in. It's our civic duty –'

" 'I'm afraid Papa wouldn't view it that

253

way,' Justin said. 'Papa would be most annoyed if we created a scene. Let me have it, Sean.'

"We argued and scuffled, and eventually he got the handkerchief. I pouted for an hour or two and then forgot it. And I didn't think of it again till Alice died and Mrs. Abbott dredged up that other murder.

"Gypsies? I wondered then. Or Justin? Hadn't he been too eager to retrieve the handkerchief? Well, it made no difference because Justin was dead. . . . Or was he? Everything fell into place: the servants, the missing picture, Aunt Margaret's desperation to be rid of Mercy. And Robin? Aunt Margaret had told me of her disappearance by then; might she not have crept away to join her fugitive husband? I questioned Mercy –"

"Very harshly," I snapped.

"Yes. I'm truly sorry for that. Anyway you interrupted – most rudely, I might add – and I was left to my own devices. I decided Justin must be at Long Hill Farm, and I planned to ride over first thing this morning. But Mr. Stowe needed me at Lakeview – he sent one of his hands with the message – and I didn't think a forenoon's delay would prove critical. As it turned out, I was dead wrong."

"So Caitlin found you at Lakeview?"

"Yes. We rode like mad to Long Hill, and

you were gone. But Hines had slipped up – your trail was clear as day in the mud – and we tore out through the woods. We didn't make it though, did we? If you hadn't got out of the coach. . . . Oh, Linnet –"

He started to kiss me, quite thoroughly. And there was a nervous cough at the door.

Giles Chapman, damn him, was early.

The rest of the week was devoted to death.

Wednesday morning: the inquest on Garrett Marlowe. As Alf had not been called, Father Stevens conducted a simultaneous graveside service for Hines and Colin. I attended only because I did not wish Alf to be alone, and after it was over, we proceeded directly to the town hall. We found the corridors abuzz with the news that the jury had returned a verdict of "willful murder."

Wednesday afternoon: the inquest on Robin Ashworth. Her body had been exhumed, but I shut my ears to the testimony of the medical examiner. Alf stumbled through his story, Caitlin acquitted herself well, and the coroner read an affidavit from Lady Margaret. The verdict was, again, murder.

Thursday afternoon: the inquest on Mary Drake. Alf had indeed forgotten "the other one," but another statement from Lady Margaret, another grim recital by Dr.

255

Reynolds, proved sufficient to yield another judgment of homicide.

Friday morning: the inquest on Harold and Colin Hines. Alf, by then, had been reduced to gibbering confusion, and it was left to me to describe the slippery road, the slithering trap. The jury's decision – quickly rendered – was accidental death.

Friday afternoon: a funeral. Mary had had no relatives, or none who could be located, and Father Stevens had proposed a double service for her and Robin. I had readily assented, and I observed Aunt Jane's shock with a macabre flicker of amusement. It makes no difference in the end, does it? I asked her silently. One was a Gentlewoman, one an orphaned servant girl, and what does it matter now? She and Uncle Henry retreated to the station as soon as decently possible.

The weekend passed in a blur. Justin was still at large, Sean told me (or was it Giles?), but he was a hunted man. There were warrants against him for the murders of Nell Smith, the dairymaid; five London prostitutes; and Alice. The city papers were demanding the head of the Shoreditch Slasher, and he would never escape, never. . . .

Alf, Caitlin, and, in absentia, Lady Margaret stood before the magistrates on

Monday. Lady Margaret's case was referred to the assizes, but Alf and Caitlin were exonerated. It was settled now, except for Justin, and now I must go to Mercy.

"I have bad news of your mama, dear," I began.

I had rehearsed all sorts of euphemisms, and I sifted among them. Robin had gone – permanently gone – but where? To America? To Australia? To heaven?

"She's dead, isn't she?" Mercy said calmly.

"Yes. Yes, she is."

"Like Papa."

How long could I protect her? And would I be protecting her or sparing myself?

"Your papa isn't dead, Mercy; your papa is very ill. And because he's ill, he's done a number of wicked things. I don't know where he is right now – no one does – but when he's found, he'll be punished. You will have to be very brave –"

"Shall I be punished as well?"

She had been my responsibility for weeks, but in that moment she became mine, and I felt a choking, dizzying rush of love. I stooped and pulled her against me, and her thin little arms stole round my neck.

"No, my darling; no, you won't. Cousin Sean and I are to be married" – had he asked me? I couldn't remember; if not, he would –

"and you will live with us. And we shall be happy; I promise you that, Mercy —"

We sobbed for a while, and then May delivered Mercy's dinner. She dribbled soup halfway across the room, but I smiled. It was absurdly, wonderfully unimportant; the dying was over.

It wasn't.

Our schedule had fallen quite apart; this was the first night we had dined together in a week. Giles and Caitlin sat on one side of the table, Sean and I on the other, and between us there flowed — how can I describe it? — a current of restrained triumph. We were, I supposed, like soldiers, soldiers who had survived a devastating enemy assault. We mourned our fallen comrades and were slightly embarrassed to find ourselves alive, but we could not suppress a primitive surge of jubilation.

Glynis — a rather pathetic outcast at the head of the table — was carping about something or other when Mrs. Abbott flew into the room.

"It's Lady Margaret," she panted. "I took her dinner down as usual, but she's — she's — well, I do fear the poor woman is —"

Dead. Several hours elapsed before Dr. Reynolds arrived and pronounced the obvious diagnosis.

Lady Margaret had suffered a second

stroke, he said. "Perhaps" – he cleared his throat – "perhaps it might be termed a – umm – blessing in view of the – umm – circumstances. Not that I should wish to suggest – umm –"

Sean and I looked at one another across the great, old-fashioned bed, and I remembered Mercy, remembered that terrible onslaught of love, and I wished Lady Margaret well.

I am tempted to describe Lady Margaret's death as the turning point – the end of the past, the beginning of the future – but I cannot. That pivotal moment had occurred just previously as we sat at table flushed, despite ourselves, with victory. For it was then we began to grasp a truth as old as man, as elusive as God: life must be drained to its dregs. It is always brief and often bitter, but it is all we have. And the day we sacrifice to Duty or Convention or any of a hundred other minor deities may be our last.

If we made this ancient but ever-startling discovery at the same time, it was Caitlin who acted on it first. We were having tea the afternoon of Lady Margaret's funeral when she announced that she and Giles would be married "as soon as legally possible." Mrs. Abbott dropped an entire tray of cucumber sandwiches.

"Miss Ashworth!" she gasped. "Perhaps you'll think me out of place, but as you've no family left to advise you. . . . Well, I must say, miss, it would be most improper, with your mother not yet cold in the ground –"

"But that is just the point, Mrs. Abbott," Caitlin interrupted tartly.

I doubt Mrs. Abbott understood, but I know the rest of us did.

Two or three days elapsed. Giles – despite a rather huffy telegram from his employers – had given no indication of returning to London. He had, in fact, taken to puttering about the gardens and riding over the estate with Sean, fairly demolishing his city wardrobe. After dinner one evening Sean invited him into the library.

I lurked across the hall in the drawing room, quivering with curiosity. Had Sean appointed himself Caitlin's protector? Was he asking all manner of stiff, paternal questions? They were beaming when they emerged from the library, and I hurriedly buried myself in a magazine.

"Did you eavesdrop?" Sean asked from the doorway.

"Certainly not," I sniffed. "Whatever transpired between you and Giles is no concern of mine –"

"Oh, but it is." He crossed the room

and sat beside me. "Giles is to assume the administration of Ashwood."

My magazine crashed to the floor. "Giles!"

"He loves the place; hadn't you noticed? I'd suspected his feelings, and tonight he confirmed them. He's the third son of a Suffolk squire, and he went to the bar only from necessity. He detests the city. He's been hoarding every farthing for years, hoping to accumulate enough to buy an estate of his own. He wasn't making much progress, he confessed, so this seems the ideal solution. I can't really picture Caitlin in London, can you? I intend to pay Giles a handsome salary, and perhaps, when Mercy reaches her majority, she'll wish to sell Ashwood. If not, Giles should be able to purchase a decent substitute." Sean beamed again.

"And what –" I framed my inquiry with great delicacy. "– what of you? You must live as well –"

"I'm not without means, Linnet."

"What – what sort of means?"

"I have investments." I said nothing. "Well, if you must know . . ."

He reeled them off with breathtaking aplomb: ownership of a bank and several textile mills, substantial holdings in a shipyard, half a dozen hotels, a publishing concern. . . . And I had thought he would kill

261

Mercy for possession of Ashwood!

"I hated it here!" he concluded passionately. "I came because I felt I had to, but I begrudged every second away from the city. I never wanted you to be Mercy's governess; I wanted you in safekeeping while I groped for a way out." He grinned. "And now that I've found it, I see no reason to wait, do you?"

"Wait for what?" I said coyly.

"Oh, for God's sake, must I ask?"

"Yes," I said demurely, "you must."

He did.

Giles and Caitlin were married on a Saturday morning; we that afternoon. Having so far defied convention, we threw all caution to the winds and held a splendid reception at Ashwood. Our guests frowned a good deal and whispered behind their hands, but – I observed – consumed enormous quantities of champagne.

Several of Giles's legal associates traveled down from London for the occasion, and at one juncture I noticed Glynis in deep conversation with a tall, bespectacled solicitor. But it was my wedding day, and we were leaving for Paris in the morning, and I thought no more about it.

As whimsical Fate would have it, Sean's London house was situated in St. James's

Street, not half a mile from Aunt Jane's. But she was not our first caller; Glynis was.

"Do you mind?" she asked rhetorically, as the cabbie wrested her interminable luggage out of the growler. "Everything has been so tiresome that I thought I deserved a holiday. . . ."

She and the scholarly Mr. Carew were married within the month.

Initially, the newspapers maintained their frantic interest in Justin. "Shoreditch Slasher Arrested in Southampton!" one headline shrilled a few months after Sean and I were married. This particular slasher proved to be a dark, bearded bank clerk, innocently emigrating to New York. Six weeks later the "Slasher" was "Located in Liverpool!" Henry Pace, an illiterate seaman with a magnificent black goatee, was released in a matter of hours. The press grew more circumspect after that – murmuring, on page two, of "potential suspects" and sundry characters who bore "a resemblance" to the Shoreditch Slasher. And eventually, new triumphs, new tragedies, crowded Justin from the papers altogether, and I ceased to look for his name.

The search continues although – Inspector Coleman has privately informed Sean – it appears futile. The police have lost all trace of Justin. He may, they say, be dead; he may successfully have emigrated; he may be living quietly in England under another assumed identity. He might not strike again for years, if, indeed, ever, and until he does . . . Until he does, we are free of him.

We frequently journey down to Ashwood, sometimes for a day, sometimes for a weekend. Alf meets us at the station, and Giles and Caitlin await us at the front door. Mercy dashes through the house and into the garden, bouncing beside her Pocahontas – the shamefully expensive doll Sean brought her from Paris. Giles, flushed with proprietary pride, spirits Sean off to tour the estate or review the books. And Caitlin and I talk of the things women have always talked of and, in recent weeks, make much over Caitlin's firstborn, a tiny, strong girl named Margaret.

"I shan't apologize," she said fiercely when she told me the name. "The moment Margaret was born, the very moment, I understood exactly why Mother did as she did."

We spoke of it again a few weeks later. Mrs. Abbott – having utterly forgotten the shocking impropriety of Caitlin's marriage – was fairly torturing the child with attention, and Caitlin and I took a stroll in the garden.

"Margaret," she mused. "Actually, I'd intended to call her Robin. Would you have objected?"

"No," I lied.

"Oh, yes, you would have." Her eyes twinkled behind her spectacles. "If Margaret had been Robin, you'd be short a name. When is yours due? Late autumn, I'd guess."

"About All Saints'," I confirmed.

"Oh, Linnet."

She hugged me, and then Mercy scampered up and the three of us trooped into the house.

All Saints'. Four months away. I'm not yet big and clumsy, and I often walk in the park and dream of unborn Robin. Robin Anne if a girl, Anne for Sean's mother; Robin John if a boy, John in memory of Father . . .

Father. I pause on the shore of the pond and gaze across it. I close my eyes, and I can almost see him: tall and spare and bent. I cock my head, and I can almost hear him: *You are not a Coachman's Daughter.*

No, Father, I am not. Nor is Glynis mistress of Ashwood nor Giles a city lawyer nor Sean a landed gentleman. No, I am not a Coachman's Daughter, but I know, at last, what I am. I am Myself.

I turn and walk away, and sometimes I think that he has heard me.